DECEIVED

DECEIVED

Peter Taylor

ROBERT HALE · LONDON

Typeset in 11/15.7pt Palatino
Printed in Great Britain by the MPG Books Group, Bodmin and King's Lynn

For Peter Henry Taylor
Your wise words and gentle ways are anchored in
our hearts and minds forever.

1

FAT STAN STOOD at the window of his upper-floor apartment, rubbed his belly and popped a tin of lager. From his vantage point he could see the Cleveland Hills to the south, the industrial landscape of Teesside to the north. He took a swig from the can, burped and permitted himself a self-satisfied smile. This was the life. It was late morning and most of the world was at work, hard at it in their boring jobs, scratching for a living. Compared to them he considered himself the emperor of Middlesbrough, lord of all he surveyed, a liberated man, not a lemming charging for the cliff with all the others, wasting away the days of their life in a repetitive cycle until finally they hit the cliff edge and tumbled into eternity. They'd never lived the life, never would. All that toil for peanuts. Well, let them take it. He'd risen above them. There were easier ways to make money if you had the guts to be different, to break out. And he'd had the guts; he'd shown them all, hadn't he?

As though to provide a fanfare to his triumphant thinking the doorbell went, playing the song which accompanied the Boro' team when they ran out at the Riverside ground on Saturdays. He did a little jig, took another swig from the can, put it down on the oak table and, wiping his fingers across his vest, padded across the thick carpet. He'd forgotten it was collection day. That must be his driver at the door. Just another bonus, wasn't it, being able to afford to have someone drive you around? Gone for ever were the days when he'd walked his patch with his thin jacket concealing the machete tied to his back, ready to use it against the lowlife street dealers who sometimes, to their cost, tried to cross him. He smiled, remembering. No more of that. Now, he was like that emperor in the story he'd heard in junior school, the one who dared go around in no clothes and nobody said a dicky bird 'cos he was the man in his territory, the need to get rough only occasional because he was amongst those in the top echelons of his trade.

There were two bolts on the door. He slid them back and opened up. Three black faces were standing there. He had time to register that one wore a beanie hat, one had dreadlocks and a third was fat, like himself. Then, deep down inside himself, he heard the warning shout which once, when his senses had been honed on the street, would have been a scream. With those senses muted he hesitated. That hesitation was enough. The one who wore the beanie hat struck him in the chest, sent him hurtling back into the hall. The other two stepped inside, grabbed his arms and ran him down the hall into the living room. They didn't hesitate, just catapulted him across the room. His head hit the fish tank as he went down. Dazed, he struggled to his knees, leaned the back of his head against the tank and looked up at the three intruders.

'You've made a big mistake,' he yelled. 'You've come to the wrong door. Get out of here or you'll be dead.'

The tall one with the dreadlocks smiled. 'No mistake. You're finished, man. New boys are in town. Time to abdicate.'

From the corner of his eye Fat Stan could see the fish swimming close to his face, mouths open, sucking in air as they stared wide-eyed at their owner. His shame and fear intermingled, vied for prominence. How could this be happening? How had his old world suddenly crossed into his new when he'd felt so secure? Why hadn't he seen it coming?

He'd seen off plenty himself as he'd risen up from the streets. In a moment of understanding he knew complacency had been his undoing. Yet he still felt hopeful that he could wriggle out of this. He had a winning hand to play because he had his money and, as always in his experience, money counted. Everyone had a price. All was not lost.

He swallowed hard. 'I'll pay you,' he whined, 'or I'll pay you tax …'

When he looked into their faces he saw amusement, knew his pleading was in vain. As they picked him up he fought them for his life, but they were strong and he'd let himself go, wasn't the same man who'd pounded the streets for hours collecting his drug money.

They opened the window, forced his head out. He felt a cold blast of air hit his face. His dressing-gown opened and the skin on his chest and arms scraped against the ledge as they pushed him out. Then his feet left the floor and his body balanced on the window sill, his stomach the fulcrum of a delicate equipoise. He kicked out with his legs like a mule, tried to resist. But he was fighting the inevitable and they launched him into space. The landscape spun, a grotesque kaleidoscope of shapes and colours as he tumbled. Before he hit the ground, just for a second a memory of the men pouring out of the factory where his father worked leapt into his mind. His last wish, before his world exploded, was that he could have been more like them.

'One down,' Dreadlocks said as they walked to the door.

'One to go,' the beanie added.

The fat one smiled. 'When we is top dogs, don't let me get as lardy as him. Thought he might bounce right back up here and bite us.'

'You already is,' Dreadlocks said and they all laughed.

2

STANDING AT THE wooden podium J P Deadman, head of the Law School at the University of Teesside raised his arms as though to reach out and embrace the audience and welcome them into his own select circle. Seated in tiers above him the third-year students looked down, some apparently hanging on his every word, others doing their best to disguise their boredom, enduring his by now familiar histrionics in the happy knowledge that this would be for the last time.

'To conclude, ladies and gentlemen,' he rumbled on, 'you go now to man the great bastion that is the law of this country, to fortify its battlements against those who would diminish it, allow anarchy a foothold in our fair land. Do it with integrity and honesty. Standing above the temptation to compromise your principles, be above the common herd for, out there in the world of men, there is weakness held within bounds only by the law.'

Deadman lowered his arms. His eyes gleamed in the strip lighting as his gaze travelled around the auditorium in expectation.

A ripple of applause, from his disappointed look clearly less than he thought his oratory merited, emerged from the ranks. It was soon superseded by the rustling of papers and shuffling of feet as the students realized he had, indeed, finished. A handful of the students, mainly those he'd tutored personally, made their way down to thank him. The majority, like a beagle pack with the whiff of freedom in its nostrils, left the auditorium and hurried off to the student coffee bar, ready for caffeine stimulation to counter the soporific effects of Deadman's drone.

James Harper, one of those at the back of the queue, was eventually served and carried his tray to a corner table where his two flatmates, who were also third-year law students, had joined his girl friend Elizabeth, a second-year business studies student. All three were guzzling iced buns.

As James lowered his six foot, heavyset frame into the chair, Dave Hickson ran a hand through his long, unruly red hair and gazed at him, a hint of mischief enlivening his bleary-eyed look.

'Right up your street, that speech,' he said, then turned his attention to Ted Sinclair, 'And yours, mate. Bet you two loved that bit about being above the common herd.'

Ted exchanged glances with Elizabeth, his cousin. James had known the two cousins since he was a child in nappies. Their families moved in the same circles. James and Ted had been inseparable at school and had agreed to study law together at Teesside University. Liz had followed a year later, her family's idea being that the two lads could watch over her.

'Count me out on this one,' Liz said, picking up a paper and raising her eyebrows disdainfully.

'Yeah! Get lost, Dave!' Ted said, licking at a piece of icing hanging off his bun.

'Deadman had a point,' James stated, taking the bait. 'He just gets carried away. Nothing wrong with the sentiment. We've finished our course. It won't be long—'

Hickson's laugh interrupted him. 'He *should* be carried away, you mean. His name tells you that. He's still up there in his ivory tower, not unlike my two flatmates, I might say.'

James flushed. 'And what exactly do you find wrong with his sentiments? Enlighten us, if you can.'

After three years of living in a flat with Hickson he knew he shouldn't have risen to the bait. Most of the three years they'd rubbed along together well enough and had become good mates. When Hickson got on his high horse, it was better just to humour him.

Hickson licked the icing off his fingers. 'That man, like you guys, has led a privileged existence. Can't you see what a snob he is? If he'd lived where I've lived, seen what I've seen, he'd understand about the "common herd" as he so insultingly puts it.'

Ted shook his head and grinned. 'An inverted snob! That's what you are Hicky.'

Unfazed, Hickson continued, 'How can he possibly make judgements. How can he temper punishment with clemency, protected as he's been in life? It's a farce to pretend he can.'

'Someone has to,' James said grumpily.

'What about you, Hicky?' Ted said mischievously. 'Can you? You've never made it clear why you went in for law.'

Hickson leaned back in his chair. 'Money, of course. It's one of the best-paid professions, isn't it?' He glanced around the room at the other students and made an expansive gesture. 'At the end of the day that's what all this lot want.'

James raised an eyebrow. 'Just money? That's it?'

'Makes the world go round, mate, and at least I know what life is like for some people, so I won't be a total mess-up. Can you two say the same, seeing as you're public-school educated and mummy and daddy have plenty of cash?'

Liz glanced up from her paper, let out a sigh. 'Give it a rest, Hicko.'

'Yes, drop it if you're going to get personal,' Ted told him.

'And by the way, we're in it for the money, but not just the money. I don't believe you are either.'

'Oh yes I am, mate. I've learned what counts in this world and it ain't Deadman's hypocrisy. Deep down that man's an élitist and I don't like élitists.'

James was doing his best to control his temper. In this mood Hickson annoyed him. He only let his resentment of those more privileged show occasionally but, when he did, he could turn nasty.

'You don't think we understand the common man, eh?' James came back at him. 'Well, we've put up with living with you for three years, haven't we?'

Without looking up, Liz said, 'Don't I just love it when two bitches fight.'

Ted tried to be placatory. 'Come on, you two. Give it a rest, can't you?'

In the embarrassing silence that followed Hickson, his face red as his hair, eyed them all in turn. When he spoke it was obvious that he was making an effort to control himself.

'I'll say this with certainty. Anyone of us would break the law if we were put in a tight enough corner, financial or otherwise. If your money, your status or your family were threatened, you'd break it. Maybe with a bad conscience, but you'd break it. If you don't believe that, life hasn't laid its hands on you yet.'

Ted, still trying to bring some levity into the proceedings, answered him with a twinkle in his eye.

'Depends on your character, old chap. We went to the right school, you know.'

Hickson, not amused, glowered. Then he glanced slyly at the other tables, made sure nobody was listening in.

'You've already broken the law. You've both taken drugs, haven't you?'

James snapped at him. 'That will stop when we leave here. Anyway, most students try them and it's under control. We're not exactly smackheads, are we?'

'But it makes my point. You've already slipped and you've had no pressure,' Hickson was sneering now, a superior look on his face.

Ted tried peacemaking again. 'Look, lads, we shouldn't be arguing. We've finished our exams. Let's enjoy the summer. We're already sounding like pedantic old men – like Deadman in fact.'

Hickson seemed to take notice this time. His mood underwent a sudden transformation. He held a hand up like a policeman on traffic duty.

'OK, fellers, I apologize. Sanctimonious people like Deadman get to me, that's all. I was wrong to take it out on you two.' He rose from his chair. 'I'll go and fetch some more coffees. Ted's right, you know. Let's have a life of hedonism before we go onwards and upwards to man that bastion of Deadman's.'

While he was at the counter Ted made a face. 'Sorry, Liz. What a bore for you. Chip on his shoulder, I'm afraid, even now that he's almost a lawyer.'

She didn't answer, just looked up from her paper at her cousin and smiled enigmatically.

James let out a long sigh. 'He's been on that theme before, but never so vehemently. Thought he would have mellowed.'

'Maybe a touch of insecurity,' Ted said. 'He knows we'll get jobs through our fathers' contacts, whereas he could struggle. This is hardly a top university and it's a competitive field out there.'

'Strange how, for all his protestations about his poor background, he's always had plenty of money,' James mused.

'He's borrowed from us a few times.'

'But he's always paid back.' James shook his head. 'Hope there's no more of his bitterness. We don't want to leave on a sour note. It would spoil the memories.'

3

WINSTON SMART STOOD on the pathway leading to a house in Linthorpe village, in the heart of Middlesbrough. His cousin had summoned him here. Bradley moved about so frequently, he wondered how long this latest address would last. Linthorpe was a pleasant place, sure enough, but his cousin could afford the best with the pile he must have stacked away. He remembered he'd told him that in his game you had to keep moving, never let them pin you down. Ostentation was out as well, no fancy clothes, no flash cars. A low profile kept you living longer, Bradley reckoned.

Walking up the path, Winston wondered why he and his cousin were so different. His own family had arrived ten years ago when he was twelve. Bradley had come over on his own a few years back, had lived in London at first. He wished he could be more like Bradley. His cousin was one of the most ruthless men he'd ever known, his character shaped by the poverty he'd left behind in Jamaica and what he'd learned as a gang member there. Winston wished he could have had that same experience to make him more like his cousin.

It was with a certain trepidation that he rang the bell. How much leeway, he wondered, would the fact that their fathers were brothers give him when it came to business. Things hadn't been going so well recently and he hoped this summons didn't augur badly for him.

Bradley opened the door, face impassive, those penetrating eyes of his moving over Winston and then beyond him. Eventually he jerked a thumb over his shoulder.

'Come,' he grunted. 'We need to talk.'

As he followed down the hall, Winston noticed the well-defined shoulder and back muscles under his cousin's grey sweat shirt. Though he was of more than average size himself, he felt small and out of condition in comparison.

They entered the living room and Bradley pointed to a chair. Winston lowered himself into it. His cousin stood over him and Winston felt physically intimidated, not just by Bradley's build but by the aura he gave off. When Bradley sat down opposite, the light from the window fell on the side of his face with the scar above the eyebrow and exaggerated the mangled ear on that side of his shaven head.

'How you doing, man?' Winston heard the chirpiness in his own voice and instantly regretted it. Everything in his cousin's demeanour had warned him it was inappropriate, that he wasn't here for social chitchat.

'Man works for me, cousin or no cousin, he gotta produce.'

Bradley's voice was chilling, stripped to the bone, nothing left on it to chew. Winston felt his muscles tensing as the rebuke penetrated.

'Been doing my best,' he said.

Bradley raised his eyebrows, inclined his head to one side. 'Best ain't good enough, then. My man tells me you been short – twice.'

Winston shifted uncomfortably in the chair. Transfixed by Bradley's stare, at first he couldn't find words. When he did find them they seemed to gurgle out of his mouth as though there was a blockage between his brain and his throat.

'Some people taking time to pay. But they do.'

'Time is money, Winston. Day comes, they won't pay at all,

17

believe me. I give you your chance 'cos our fathers are brothers. But business is business. Why should I get sentimental just 'cos my father far away in Jamaica ask if I can do you a favour?'

Winston lowered his eyes, fixed them on the carpet. He didn't think he'd been doing that badly. He'd been making a profit, hadn't he? It was true a few of the dealers he ran owed him but they always paid up in the end. Unless he'd missed the drift here, his cousin was ready to dispense with his services and it pained him to think about that; after all, this was the best money he'd earned in his life. There was nothing for it but to eat a piece of humble pie and hope it would satisfy Bradley.

'Give me another chance. I won't let you down.'

Bradley sighed. 'Whisper is you being soft. That's why they dragging things. That's why you a few thousand behind. You cane them, they soon pay up. Know what I mean, man?'

'If that's what you want, Bradley.'

Bradley shook his head. 'It's not what I wants. It's how it works, a built-in factor, bro. But I don't know if you got it in you. You're not like me. I never took no rubbish from nobody. It all 'bout respect man, end of day.'

Winston felt the blood rush to his face. The words were humiliating, a lash laid on his back, as if his manhood was being questioned. If his cousin wanted him to do damage for him, he had it in him. He knew he had. For sure, he was no stranger to violence. Yardie blood ran in his veins, even though he'd been long gone from Jamaica.

'I got the message. Jus' give me 'nother chance. I won't let you down, man.'

'Better not, Winston. Otherwise, I take you off the payroll.'

For a moment they stared into each other's eyes, like animals at a waterhole understanding where lines were drawn that couldn't be crossed. Bradley's cold stare spoke volumes. It told his cousin to take him very seriously, that this was his last chance and, if he had to, he would cast him adrift without a second thought. It was Winston who broke the spell and looked away.

Bradley spoke again. 'Your father, he OK?'

'Sweet, man.'

Bradley rose from the chair, stretched his massive frame. 'Well, don't be letting him down. You make him some money. Our fathers knew bad times back in the day, uh?'

'They surely did.'

Understanding, without it being said, that business was finished and it was time for him to leave, Winston started for the door, Bradley following him.

On the threshold, before he closed the door, Bradley said, 'I won't be using this place again. Maybe I get a country place.'

As he closed the gate behind him, Winston was doing some serious thinking. Though it hurt his pride to admit it, maybe Bradley was right in reprimanding him. His cousin was the man, wasn't he? Knew the business inside out. By his standards, he was probably being a pussy cat. It was a fact that, if people owed you, they should pay up, no messing. Perhaps some of the dealers working for him were taking him for a ride. Make an example or two and the others would think twice. It was all about respect, just like Bradley had said. Winston decided, then and there, that he was going to get some for himself.

4

DAVE HICKSON OPENED the door, popped his head out, and with slow deliberation, like a spy about to emerge from hiding, scanned the street. It was late afternoon and there was nobody about. He considered this ritual a bit of an unnecessary rigmarole because he knew James and Ted were booked on the university squash courts and wouldn't be back for another hour, not unless they had a change of mind. Yet, he had to admit to himself, the little bit of chance involved added a touch of excitement to his deceit.

Glancing over his shoulder, he watched Elizabeth adjusting her blonde hair in the hall mirror, wondered whether the secrecy of their trysts added spice for her too. Watching her now he thought, not for the first time, that he could detect a touch of the aristocrat in her, in the way she held herself, that tilt of the head which seemed to announce to the world that nothing it could do would shake an inner confidence. Or was it an assumed superiority? Was it bred into her from birth or had it developed in the refined circles in which her family moved, he wondered? Had that been the attraction for him? The attraction of opposites, desiring what you could never be yourself. Whatever it was, none of the girls back home had it, that was for sure. Then again, none of those girls back home had her moneyed background. A man might gain in life with her by his side, he mused. High maintenance she might be, but she'd be an asset to her partner in any business, would know how to entertain, how to impress.

'Coast's clear, down periscope,' he announced. 'No torpedoes in the water.'

'Don't be too flippant,' she said, applying her lipstick. 'It isn't nice, what we're doing.'

He laughed. 'Wondrous is the mind of woman.'

She made to step round him but he reached out, caught her in his arms. She threw back her head, looked down her nose at him in the way he found so appealing.

'I'm not flippant where you're concerned,' he told her, grasping her chin between his thumb and fingers as he looked into her eyes. 'You're going to have to choose one day, you know, James or me.'

'Will I, now?' she came back at him.

He forced a smile. 'You like what we're doing, don't you? Like the sneaking around. Brings a bit of excitement into your life.'

She pushed his arms away. 'You're wrong! I don't! James has been good to me all the time I've known him. I'm just undecided about some things, things to do with me – not him.'

'If you have doubts, end it with him. The longer you leave it the worse it'll be.'

'Another month,' she said. 'What harm? You'll all be moving on, somewhere else. It'll be the test.'

He glowered. 'I'll still be in the frame, won't I, if you finish with him?'

She stroked his cheek with a long finger. 'Just wait and see, Dave. Don't push me. Right now I've got a lecture to attend. It's all right for you, swanning around. I've still another year to do, remember.'

As she left the house he fought back his anger. 'We'll meet again, don't know where, don't know when,' he sang, in a mock Vera Lynn voice 'But I know we'll meet again some sunny day.'

She called over her shoulder. 'That's what I like about you, Dave. You've got old-fashioned sentiments – I don't think.'

He waved her off in her car, then went inside, harbouring vague stirrings of discontent. He realized, when he'd argued with James in the coffee bar that morning, that he had gone too far, probably out of his frustration with Elizabeth because she wouldn't end it with his flatmate. Deep down, he didn't really care whether James found out about them or not. Another month and, as Liz had mentioned, they'd be leaving Teesside, so it wouldn't make much difference if he found out. He'd enjoyed living and studying with James and Ted but time moved people on. There wasn't much they could give him now. With Liz it was different. She had a lot to give, yet he couldn't be sure of her. She was having a fling with him, but he had the sneaking suspicion she'd be staying with James when it came right down to it. His own appeal, he sensed, lay in the difference between him and her usual circle, in that streetwise wisdom which made him seem more mature, the risk-taker in him. Would it be enough to keep her? He couldn't help doubting it. Sometimes, he felt he was just an experiment, a bit of rough on the side before she settled down, so that she could imagine she'd lived a bit. Whatever, he knew that, under that veneer of sophistication, she was as devious in her own way as he was himself. If only she could see they'd be good together.

5

IN THE EVANESCENT light, D I Harry Davis stood on the bank of the River Tees, stared at the smoke belching out of the industrial chimneys, the long tongues of red flames shooting up at the black clouds chasing across the heavens. He'd read somewhere that this was the view that had been used in the film Blade Runner to represent a bleak, futuristic landscape. Tonight, with the grotesque vision a few yards away and the dark, fathomless water ruffling in the wind just beyond it, he wondered if this wasn't more like the banks of the mythical river Styx, the staging post for Hell.

He knew what they said about policemen: that, like doctors, they developed a black sense of humour as a coping device, a shield against the horrors they had to witness, but right now he couldn't dredge up a morsel of humour. He knew why. It was those eyes staring up at him, not because he hadn't seen his share of dead eyes before, but because those eyes belonged to a head lying a few feet away, a head which had been severed from its body.

One of the SOCO team crossed his line of vision, jerked a thumb over his shoulder. 'We found the rest of him down river,' he said, in a matter-of-fact tone, 'with both arms chopped off.'

DC Diane Harland came up beside Davis. He was surprised how well she was bearing up, probably better than he was if truth were told. He figured it was the fact that he could put a name to that decapitated head, humanize it, even though its former owner hardly rated high in the scale of humanity, that gave him his disadvantage. For as sure as sin, that face belonged to a man he detested, a man whom many would say deserved a far worse fate than decapitation and would have liked to deliver the cutting blow themselves if they'd had the bottle.

'Jack Hudson,' he murmured as he turned his collar up against the gathering breeze. 'The rest of him is further along the bank without his arms.'

Harland stared at him, an incredulous look on her face. 'You can tell who he is?' She paused, pointed at the head. 'From that!'

'Hardly more monstrous in death than in life, all things told.'

Harland blew out her cheeks. 'Must have been one ugly man.'

'About on par with your current boyfriend, I'd say – in the looks department that is.'

For a moment she thought he was serious, glared in his direction. He smiled and said, 'Just my attempt to find my sense of humour.' Then he added, in an avuncular tone, 'Don't worry, I know your taste's impeccable, Diane.'

She lost the glare. 'How do you know him?'

'Drug boss, but clever, very clever. Learned never to dirty his own hands. Probably he'd have slipped up in the end, but he was laughing at us.'

'Well, he's stopped laughing now.'

Two of the SOCO team went past them and headed further up the bank. They glanced at the head and at their other colleagues working at the ground near by.

'Got a head start on us,' Davis heard one of them remark.

'Yeah! But they reckon ours is an 'armless old chap,' the other came back at him quick as a flash.

The two detectives groaned, then were quiet for a moment until Harland said, 'Sir, do you think this is related to—'

'Good chance,' he said, interrupting her. 'One drug boss, Fat Stan, takes flying lessons and lands on his head, the other has his cut off, and all in the space of two days. Looks like someone's sending out messages. Let's hope I'm wrong, but I'd say it's shaping that way.'

Harland shook her head. Now that Davis was growing used to the gruesome find and what it said about the dark ones who moved amongst his own species in the disguise of humans, he studied her more closely, realized she was more perturbed than she'd appeared, was putting up a good front.

'Vicious bastards,' she hissed. 'Thousands of years of civilization and this is the result.'

He wanted to tell her that there were plenty of good people in the world, not to lose sight of that or the job could unhinge her. He knew that she needed to know, as he had himself when he was her age, what some men were capable of. It wouldn't be often she'd come across scenes like this one but just knowing about them would help her understand why their job counted, why the lid had to be held down.

'Worse to come,' he said. 'Can feel it in my old bones.'

He glanced at the head and the men working near it with such meticulous care, like acolytes performing worshipful rites on holy ground marked off by the yellow demarcation tape.

'Let's get out of here,' he said. 'We'll come back later when SOCO have done their thing.'

In spite of the fact it was summer the wind was cold and it was a relief to get back in the car. Harland was quiet and it allowed him to mull things over as he drove. He didn't like what he sensed brewing. Last week, one of the more co-operative toms whom he used for information had told him the word was that some of the street girls were being offered what she euphemistically termed party packs by their dealers. The party packs, she'd informed him, consisted of a bag of smack and two free rocks. It didn't take much of a brain to figure out the reason for the generosity. In the blink of an eye, the girls would be hooked on crack. You could bet your life there'd be no more freebies after that. The dealers' party piece would be to force the girls, once they were hooked, to sell to their punters. Money and greed was what it was about and damnation for anybody in the way. Disgusted by the insidious evil, he banged his fist on the steering wheel. Wondering what was happening, Harland sat bolt upright.

'What's up, sir?'

'Speaking to the devil,' he said. 'He's telling me we've seen what he can do and there'll be more lives harmed.'

6

THE THREE FLATMATES sat around the table in companionable silence. It was weekday night and the Blacksmith's Arms was emptying. People were leaving because they had to work the next day. The flatmates didn't, and that was why, if they hadn't yet reached the incoherent stage, they were a little the worse off for drink. The session had helped assuage any resentment which might have lingered from the argument earlier in the day, concerning Deadman and his pontificating; normal conviviality had been restored with the aid of Newcastle Brown ale.

'The night is still young,' James said, one eye on the barman circling them as he collected empty glasses. 'And we're young and handsome with time to kill.'

'There's a dance at the student's union,' Ted announced.

Hickson stared into his glass, swirled the contents. 'Just think,' he said dolefully, 'another year and they won't let us into the dance. Be past our sell-by date at twenty-two.'

James grinned. 'We're twenty-two, Dave. You are twenty-five, remember. Way past your sell-by date.'

'Seriously, we should go,' Ted said. 'It'll be the last time. Make hay while the sun is still shining and all that.'

'You two will be all right, won't you?' Hickson said, sounding sorry for himself. 'From now on it'll be hunt balls, dicky bow ties, horsey women, chinless wonders. Tally ho!'

Ted giggled. 'James and Elizabeth Harper will lead off with the first waltz.'

James laughed along with his friend, then suddenly his facial muscles tightened.

'Not so sure that's an accurate prophecy,' he said. 'Liz has been a bit funny recently. Doesn't see me as much and makes work the excuse all of a sudden.'

Dave, knowing the reason for her vacillations, was secretly pleased. James's bad news was his good news where Liz was concerned. He decided it was a matter best not pursued. He diverted the conversation.

'Ted's right. Let's head down to the dance.'

Checking that the landlord wasn't looking, he reached inside his jacket pocket, withdrew a small bottle and unscrewed the top. He poured two white pills on to his palm and gave them to James and Ted, who grabbed them and put them in their mouths.

James took a swig of beer. Looking a trifle guilty, he said, 'That's the last time for me. I appreciate it, mate, but it's not a habit I want to take away with me.'

'Me neither,' Ted added.

'If Liz found out, she'd kill me,' James mused.

Dave grunted. He knew Liz better, didn't he? She'd been quite willing to try drugs at his instigation. At that private school she'd attended she'd not come across any, which he considered a minor miracle in this day and age. Yet she was restrained in her usage, didn't let it rule her life. He admired her for that, the way she controlled it, maintaining that cool, calculating manner even as she indulged. He wondered whether part of his attraction for her was that he indulged and had an ever ready supply. Was it the novelty, the excitement of the forbidden? If she really knew the extent of his activities, maybe she wouldn't be so keen.

'Need the toilet, lads,' he announced. 'This twenty-five-year-old can't rave on a full bladder.'

The landlord, who was hovering over a nearby table, heard his remark. 'Use the toilet out back, will you son? Some dirty pig has blocked up the one at the front. Only be careful because there's no lights back there.'

'Any loo will do,' Dave said and giggled as he started for the back door.

The yard was dark and cobbled. Off to his right he could see a faint light at the end of the long alley which was like a tunnel leading to the street at the front of the pub. He glanced up at the sky. There were no stars out and a crescent moon wasn't giving out much light.

Afraid he might stumble, he took his time traversing the cobbles. He made it to the door, reached down to feel for the handle. That was when he sensed somebody standing close to him. He reeled back, half-turned, peered at the shape not a yard away from him. He saw that it had human form but it was too dark to make out the face or any features. It seemed to be just one hulking mass. The small child in him, the one that had been afraid of imaginary bogeymen, stirred. The creature, for that is what it seemed to be to him, stood silently, like something that had metamorphosed out of the blackness into human form, yet seemed to lack the vital soul to make it human. Dave felt his spine tingle with apprehension, heard his breathing accelerate.

Without warning, the creature reached out, grabbed his jacket, spun him round, sent him crashing against the stone wall. His arm was thrust up his back. He thought it must be near to breaking because the pain was unbearable. The creature's face moved close to his. He could smell the garlic on its breath, intermingled with the smell of urine emanating from the toilet. That foul odour and the taste of his own fear made him want to vomit. But much worse was his sense of

29

helplessness against the sheer physical threat the creature represented. What was happening here?

'Take me for a fool?'

Strangely, the words gave him hope, a measure of relief. The creature had a human voice, was communicating. Better still, he recognized the voice and thought he could negotiate his way out of this situation. He'd always managed to appease the owner of that voice in the past. He wasn't exactly the brightest button.

'No, man! What makes you think—?'

A fist in his ribs knocked the breath out of him, cut off his question. What was wrong with the guy? He'd never been violent before. Wriggling out of this wasn't going to be as easy as he'd hoped.

As he gasped for air, he felt something metallic pressed against his neck. He was sure it was a gun. His bowels rumbled and his heart started to pump faster. Was this it? Was his life going to end here in this stinking back alley, the bullet poised at the end of that gun barrel the final arbiter of his destiny.

'You don't turn up with my money. You dis' me again.'

'Don't worry, you'll get it,' Dave groaned. 'I'm just a bit short.'

'That's what you said before.'

'Please, man – just need a week. I promise—'

'Now!' the voice rasped.

Dave heard something in the voice different from the other times, an implacability, as though its owner had found another personality, one which had set out on a quest and, no matter what, was determined to see it through. He feared that his words, his excuses, would be blunt weapons against whatever was driving his aggressor. But his survival instinct made him try.

'You know I don't carry money like that. Nobody does,' he groaned. 'But you'll get it. I swear you will.'

'Same old song. Sick of hearing it. You got to learn respect.'

He felt the gun barrel move away from his neck. Just for a moment he dared to hope his ordeal was over, that this was all done to scare him. The gun barrel striking the side of his head soon disabused him of that notion. His knees gave way and he slid down the wall. Bizarrely, he was grateful he hadn't been shot. A knee connected with his head, sent him sprawling his length on the cobbles and he forgot about gratitude. As though he was a sack of rubbish, strong hands reached down, pulled him to his feet. His thoughts spun in a vortex of pain and confusion. Had this Neanderthal spared him the bullet only to beat him to the point of death? Or until he was dead? What could he do? He remembered James and Ted. Where were they? Maybe they could stop this.

He was vaguely conscious of the wall behind him. A blow bounced his head against it, then another, until a curtain started to descend. He fought against it but it was a losing battle. Just before it engulfed him, somewhere out there in the ether he heard a voice, like a distant echo.

'This is me,' the voice was saying. 'I've done pussyfootin'. You're seeing the man in me now. I jus' never let him out before.'

7

THE LANDLORD WAS hovering. It was clear, though he wasn't saying it, that he wanted to close up for the night. James glanced at his watch, then towards the door.

'What's keeping him?'

Ted scratched the back of his head. 'Beats me. Could have started his own water company by now.'

James stood up 'He always did dribble on. Let's go out that way. It makes no odds.'

They said goodnight to the landlord who followed them to the door. As soon as they stepped out the lights in the pub were extinguished and they heard the bolt drawn behind them. Clearly, the landlord was ready for his bed.

At first, standing there in the dark, they couldn't see very much, but they could hear noises too loud for rats. It focused their attention on a spot near the toilets.

A hint of anxiety in his voice, James called out, 'Dave? Is that you?'

When his eyes adjusted, the anxiety shot up the scale. He could make out two shapes across the yard. He knew those shapes were men and, even though he couldn't make out features, their body language spoke volumes; one of the men was threatening the other; his fist was drawn back as though to strike; the intended recipient was against the wall, sagging at the knees, like a puppet on slack strings.

A light went on in the upstairs living-quarters, casting enough light on the proceedings to enable them to recognize Dave as the victim. His head was lolling to one side as though he was right out of it. Both students rushed across the yard. Without hesitating, James reached out, caught the bigger man's arm before it could deliver another blow.

The man shook him off and, still holding Dave up, turned his head towards them. They saw anger flaring in a black face. He looked them up and down, but obviously didn't consider them a threat because he just turned back to his task and dismissed them with snarled warning.

'On your way. Me and this boy got business.'

Like novice soldiers under a heavy bombardment for the first time and in awe of its magnitude, they were rooted to the spot while the fist struck home. They saw Hickson's head bounce against the wall. Then the fist struck again, and his eyelids fluttered like butterfly wings.

Fear and helplessness engulfed James. A voice in his head was screaming for him to do something! Anything! But he was paralysed. This savageness was outside anything he'd ever known, the wanton horror of it beyond the bounds of his civilized world. Somewhere from the dark recesses of his mind the word coward bored its way towards the light, challenged his manhood. His shame driving him, he looked around for a weapon. All he could see was a pile of bricks on the ground near the entrance to the alley. He picked one up and, steeling himself, rushed at the man, hit him on the back of his head twice in succession as hard as he could.

The man released Dave, stood as still as a monolith for what seemed an age, then shook his shoulders. James watched, horrified at what he'd done and afraid, too, because his blows appeared to have had only minimal effect. The man was starting to turn his bulk towards him, his limb movements as ponderous as a tormented bear seeking its attacker. James was sure it was going to be his turn next for a beating. All his instincts told him to flee. But, as though held in thrall, he was rooted to the spot. Fortunately, Ted found his courage, picked up a brick, lifted it high and struck. This time the man cried out, went down on to one knee. For a moment it looked as though he was going to topple. Then, like a boxer who appears finished but finds the strength to beat the count, he rose from the cobbles, reached out for the wall to steady himself. Without even turning to look at the two students he staggered towards the alley. They stood in silence until, like a creature manufactured in the realms of darkness returning to its source, he vanished from their sight.

James and Ted stared at each other, both breathing hard. James could hardly believe what they had done, that within seconds an enjoyable night out had turned into such horror. Neither spoke of it as they turned towards Dave, who was lying prone near the wall and not moving.

James bent over him, felt the pulse in his neck, looked up at Ted who was shaking.

'He's alive, thank God!'

Ted's voice was so dry it was a rasp. 'We have to ring for an ambulance.'

He reached inside his coat, brought out his mobile, struggled to quell the quivering in his fingers. As he began to dial James reached for his arm and restrained him.

'Think a minute. There's no witnesses here. How will this look? If the police find that guy, he's going to accuse us. Our word against his.'

'No way, man. We were right. We were defending Dave.'

James swallowed hard 'We hit him so hard – too hard. Undue force. You know how it goes – only enough force.'

Ted's brow wrinkled. His mouth dropped open as another

thought, another obstacle, struck him. 'We've drugs in our bloodstream and Dave could well have too. If the police test—'

He didn't have to say more. The shock of the encounter had been bad enough but now the full implications were sinking in for both of them.

'This could ruin our careers.' James said. 'Even if we come through it, the doubt will remain. Students high on drugs and all that. It'll be a stain that won't rub out.'

Ted dropped his head, mumbled, 'It could look bad, couldn't it? People will wonder.'

They stared down at Hickson who still hadn't moved. They would have to do something and quickly. Time was wasting.

'He could die—' James said.

Ted held up his mobile. 'We have to ring!'

But James's mind was in overdrive, looking for a way out. He gripped Ted's arm tight.

'Look, we don't have to hang around. We can just report it and get out of here.'

There was a flicker of hope in Ted's face but only for a second. He stared at James incredulously.

'Leave the scene! Leave! That's mad, man! We'd be found out. Then we'd really look guilty, wouldn't we?'

As though he was attempting to convince himself as much as Ted, James voiced the thoughts as they came to him.

'Dave was out of it. He didn't know what was happening. I'm nearly sure of that. We can explain to him later if we have to. He'll back us if it comes to it. We did it for him.'

'The landlord,' Ted said. 'What about the landlord? He knows we were together. God, why are we even discussing this? We have to get Dave help right now.'

'It was dark,' James persisted, firing his words rapidly. 'We left the pub, couldn't see him in the toilet. We headed home thinking he must have done the same. Somehow we missed him lying there – if he was there.'

'OK! OK! That's what we'll do. Now just let me ring.'

'Don't use your own phone. They could trace it.' James snapped as Ted began to dial. He bent down, took Dave's mobile from his pocket, handed it to Ted. 'Use this one. We'll hide it later. They'll think he was mugged for it.'

Ted saw the logic, added his own precaution by putting his handkerchief over the mouthpiece to disguise his voice. Then he rang the emergency services, refused to give his name and stressed the need to hurry. While he was talking, James took off his jacket and used it to wrap up the bricks.

'Let's go,' Ted said, starting to move towards the alley.

'Not that way,' James told him, making towards a gate at the back of the yard, the bricks under his arm. 'We'll use the back way out. It's quieter, no CCTV.'

They'd just stepped out through the gate when James pulled up short, pushed the bundle of bricks into Ted's arms.

'What now?' Ted complained.

'One second,' James said and turned back.

He crossed the yard, went through Hickson's pockets, found the small bottle. Without pausing he unscrewed the top and hurled the contents into the alley. He considered it was the least they could do for Dave; there wouldn't be any drugs on him when they took him to hospital.

As they hurried home through the dark back streets avoiding people, consumed by guilt and terrified of the consequences of their actions, James said, 'We'll get rid of the bricks and hide that phone somewhere. After that we should be in the clear.'

8

AN HOUR LATER, back in the flat, drained of energy and over-whelmed by the course of events, James and Ted sat hunched over mugs of black coffee. They'd cleaned the blood off the bricks, thrown them in the bushes at the end of the back garden. Ted suggested hiding the phone in a cavity in their garden wall, a place which they'd used in the past to hide a spare key. Unable to think of anywhere else at the moment, James had gone along with the idea.

James studied his friend closely. Ted was staring into the far corner of the kitchen with a bleak expression, as though he was foreseeing vistas of trouble which he'd be lucky to traverse unscathed. Suddenly, shaking his head, he spoke out in a voice like a lost child's. It seemed to address his own conscience as much as his friend.

'I can't believe what I just did.'

James held his counsel for a moment. He'd always known he was the more robust of the two of them, mentally and physically, more of a leader really. Whatever happened now, he knew it was important that they held their nerve. It was too late to turn back. What was done was done. You made a decision and stuck with it or you were a ditherer, no use to anybody. No way did he feel good about it himself, but he was more worried about Ted's state of mind, knew that he was going to have to be the one to pilot them through this maelstrom which had come unbidden into their lives.

'If we keep our heads we'll be all right, Ted.'

Ted slammed his fist down on to the table. 'If only we hadn't taken those damn pills we could have stayed there with him.' His voice rose in panic. 'What if they can't find him? What if he … dies?'

'They'll find him. Your directions were precise. And don't forget we hit that guy hard. How could that be construed? There'd be room for doubt, wouldn't there?'

A solitary tear hovered precariously on Ted's eyelash. 'We thought about ourselves,' he said, with a sigh. 'We should have stayed, trusted we'd come out of it all right. We should have trusted the law, trusted … justice.'

James was having his own doubts and Ted's words plucked at his conscience. Yet he still believed dissociating themselves from the nasty business had been the best practical option. In any case, Ted was looking at the worst-case scenario, needed to be lifted out of that pessimism or he'd crack. They had the brains, the two of them, to overcome this.

'Look, the most likely thing is that Dave will turn up here tomorrow with a bandage on his head and shouting the odds like he always does. As for the black guy, he was still on his feet, so probably he went off to lick his wounds and won't report anything because he knows he was the instigator.'

The optimistic way James laid it on the line lifted Ted's mood a little. He wiped his eyes with his sleeve and met James's gaze.

'Do you think it was a mugging?'

James looked pensive, then shrugged. 'Who knows? We know Dave dabbled in drugs, albeit in a very small way. At least, that's what he always told us. Just bought for his own use and a few friends. Maybe he got involved with some unsavoury character from that world, offended him in some way. Then again, perhaps it's something entirely unrelated, random perhaps.'

'I hope to God it unravels the best way for all of us,' Ted said, a perplexed look on his face.

James drained his coffee, glad that his friend seemed to have gained control of himself.

'We need to get our story right, Ted, be in complete agreement, so that if there's any surprises there'll be no room to suspect us. We just missed Dave in the dark, that's all. We have to stress that, never waver from it.'

Ted nodded agreement and they spent the next half-hour going over it, looking for loopholes in their alibi, refining it. Then, exhausted, they dragged themselves to bed.

James, in spite of his mental and physical exhaustion, couldn't get to sleep. Events in that back alley kept replaying in his brain. When he'd struck that black man over the head with the brick, he'd encountered a part of himself he didn't like. Had it been a cowardly act on his part? Why couldn't he have just grappled with the attacker? Ted would have helped to overpower him physically and they could have sent him on his way with no more than a bit of a beating? Using a brick on the skull was a different matter. Had he resorted to that because, for the first time in his life, he'd come up against something he couldn't control? Was that the real reason he'd wanted to walk away from it? He hoped not, hoped it was for a more pragmatic reason, the one he'd given Ted, rather than just pure shame at encountering the uncivilized primitive he hadn't suspected lurked inside him. His only consolation was that he'd had to do something to save Dave and that Ted had reacted the same way as he had.

9

HARRY DAVIS FOLDED his elbows on the desk, shut his eyes to give them a rest. He was in the operations room dedicated to the two recent murders. The team were at their own desks, working flat out because there was a perceived danger of escalated gang warfare on the streets of Middlesbrough as a consequence of the recent killings. Their work would be increasingly under the spotlight too, and Harry knew the usual critics would crawl out of the woodwork to lambaste the team for incompetence as the pressure piled up. This morning he'd been concentrating hard on Fat Stan's big fall from grace, going through what the uniformed guys had discovered from the house-to-house calls, one tedious detail after another.

Like a needle mark on a junkie's arm, one fact stood out amongst a host of trivialities; someone had noticed three black men getting into a car two streets away from Stan's residence; couldn't swear it but thought it was approximately around the time of his death. In itself, that wouldn't have meant much, not normally, but taken alongside the gruesome methods of killing, it aroused Davis's suspicions. Of course, he knew the dangers of making assumptions, but he couldn't resist the word hammering at his brain with all the persistence of a woodpecker's beak at full throttle. That word was 'Yardies' and he was familiar with all its connotations. Those gangsters, originating in the back yards of the West Indies towns and villages, had a reputation for extreme violence. In the past they'd operated in Middlesbrough, dealing crack cocaine on a small scale, not on the same level as in London or even places in Scotland and Wales. They'd been held in check in his town but Davis couldn't help wondering whether the recent murders were the beginning of a large scale incursion?

Davis opened his eyes found DC Harland standing in front of him, hands behind her back, looking nonplussed, as though she didn't want to disturb his stolen moment.

'Just slipped away to a peaceful place,' he said, grinning. 'And now I awake to my nightmare.'

She flicked her blonde hair out of her eyes. 'Dark forces brought me here,' she said. 'The drug unit told me there was an attack on a student last night in the back yard of the Blacksmith's Arms. He was badly hurt and they found ecstasy near the scene.'

Davis shrugged. 'And that has some relevance, has it?'

With a smug look Harland brought her hands from behind her back and placed a CCTV tape on the desk.

'When I looked at this, I thought it might.'

He eyed the cassette. 'Save me watching it. Elaborate, Diane.'

'It shows a black gent, sir, not far from the pub at approximately the time they believe the student was beaten up. The thing is, he's in a bad way – staggering all over the place.'

Davis's interest flickered into life but, on reflection, he couldn't find much there to sustain it. A possible West Indian, probably drunk, didn't constitute Yardie connections. Pure coincidence was more likely. After all, there were plenty of decent West Indians in the town.

'And that's it, Diane? That's why you look like your boyfriend's just found it in his heart to propose.'

She didn't retaliate. 'When they zoomed in, sir, they noticed he was badly injured, blood all over his face, down his shirt. The local chip-shop owner confirmed it, saw him staggering past his shop like a man on his last legs. Left a bloodied hand-mark on the fellow's window so they're checking DNA.'

Davis's interest revived but there was not enough to it to really get him going. If the student and this guy had a fight, it was more likely to do with ecstasy found nearby than the crack cocaine being whispered about on the street. Yet, it might be worth a look. There was precious little else to go on at the moment.

'The student is in hospital, is he?'

'Yes, sir, James Cook Hospital. He's in a bad way. Can't remember a thing about the attack but he knows his name and other things. They think it's amnesia but don't know if it's temporary or not. They think he'll be OK with rest.'

'Who found him?'

'That's the strange thing, sir. The call to the emergency services was made on a phone registered to him but they couldn't find it at the scene and the fellow on the CCTV didn't look capable of making the call.'

'A violent mugger with a conscience to make the call doesn't fit either,' Davis mused. He wondered how far he should bother with this, how much energy he could afford to expend on something that in all probability had no connection with his priorities. Yet he'd seen cases before where a stone had been left unturned and the investigators regretted it later, so he made his decision to give it time.

'See if you can get the face blown up, then pass it round,' he told Harland. 'When I've gone through a few more of these infernal statements I might have a run out to the Blacksmith's Arms and speak to the landlord. Could do with some fresh air.'

Looking pleased with herself, Harland lifted up the tape and started to walk away.

'Well done,' he called after her. 'Worth interrupting my beauty sleep for, wasn't it?'

She turned, gave him a wicked grin. 'If that's what it was for, get lots of sleep, sir; lots of it.'

10

JAMES STOOD UP, went to the window and looked out on the grey day. Swollen clouds, as ominous as the thoughts that had plagued him all night, trundled across the sky. It was afternoon and he was still in his dressing-gown. Ted, similarly attired, was seated at the kitchen table sipping his second cup of black coffee. As James sat down beside him, glazed eyes peered at him with a dreamlike vagueness.

'We haven't heard anything about Dave,' Ted muttered.

'No doubt we will. Keep your nerve, old son.'

James reached towards the coffee pot, froze mid-motion when the doorbell rang. Ted heard it and his body jerked upright as though he'd been struck by an uppercut from an unseen opponent. Their eyes converged in a moment of mutual apprehension.

'This is it,' Ted said, grimacing. 'Nobody calls this time of day.'

James made an effort to compose himself, got out of the chair. As he did so, at the edge of his vision a bird, which must have perched on the window sill, suddenly launched itself. Its flapping wings startled him and did nothing for his attempt at composure.

'What are we going to say?' Ted whined.

James frowned his disapproval. 'Get a grip, man! We went over it enough times. If I have to invite someone in, everything has to look normal. If it's about Dave, as far as we know he's still in bed after a late night.'

The bell rang again. James knotted his dressing-gown belt. Breathing deeply in an effort to steady his nerves, he opened the kitchen door and started down the hall.

He opened the front door to a caller dressed in a dark-blue suit, white shirt and patterned tie. The man's hair was steel-grey and cut very short, so that it emphasized a round, middle-aged face. Noticing his briefcase, James's first impression was that he was a salesman. He was ready to be irritable; sales talk was the last thing he needed today. The visitor smiled, flashed a warrant card. James's heart started to pump harder; the moment of truth had arrived.

'Detective Inspector Davis,' a surprisingly pleasant voice announced in a Teesside accent. 'I'm making enquiries about a Dave Hickson who, I believe, resides here. May I come in for a moment?'

James felt the vomit rise in his stomach, tasted it in his mouth. He fought it down and stood aside.

'Sure, come in, Inspector. Dave's our flatmate. There's three of us share. I'm James. Ted's in the kitchen. Excuse the dressing-gown. I'm afraid we're not long up. Heavy session last night, I'm afraid.'

He sensed he was rambling like an old woman. The policeman was just smiling, an adult indulging a child, so he shut up and led him down the hall to the kitchen.

'Ted, this is Detective Inspector Davis,' he announced as they entered, hoping his friend would manage to mask his feelings. 'It's something to do with Dave.'

James watched Ted carefully. To his relief, he looked at the policeman with a steady gaze and, when he spoke, his voice was strong enough, betraying no sign of nerves.

''Morning, Inspector. Dave's probably still in bed. I'll get him for you, shall I?'

'He won't be in bed, son.'

The policeman leaned against the sink. In the ensuing silence, James tried to look perplexed. He could hear a steady dripping from the tap into the plastic washing-up bowl. In his state of heightened awareness it sounded like an executioner's drum roll. He sensed that Davis was watching and weighing them like a farmer measuring the merits of livestock for the slaughter.

'I'm afraid your friend, Dave Hickson, was badly beaten up last night. He's in James Cook Hospital right now.'

'My God,' James said, putting as much surprise into his voice as he could muster. 'How – how bad is he?'

'He should be OK. The worst of it is some of his memory has been affected, a form of amnesia, the doctors say.'

'Thank God it's no worse,' Ted joined in. 'It must have been a mugging.'

Davis shook his head. 'He still had his wallet and there was money in it. His address was in his wallet which is how we knew he lived here.'

'Someone with a grudge?' James suggested.

A half-smile played on the detective's lips. 'Doing my job for me, are you, son? First a mugging, then a grudge.'

'We're law students,' James came back at him without hesitation. 'Habit of ours – playing with possibilities, asking questions.'

Davis shot him a knowing glance. 'Don't forget defending the indefensible.'

The detective let that sink in then turned his gaze on Ted. 'Obviously you haven't a clue about what happened or you wouldn't be thinking he's still in bed.'

'We were in the pub last night,' Ted explained. 'Dave left us to go to the toilet. When he didn't return we thought he'd just gone home to bed.'

'Didn't think to check the toilet?'

'We called out but there was no reply. It was dark in the back yard and Dave has left us like that before. We'd had a good drink. That doesn't always lead to sensible thinking.'

Davis nodded thoughtfully. 'I know you had a good bevvy. I've already spoken to the landlord.'

'All three of us had,' Ted told him.

'It does seem a bit strange though, because your friend was found in that back yard and you didn't see him.'

'Not really strange, Inspector.' James said. 'You see, that yard is darker than a dungeon at night, so dark it's rarely used. Easy to miss someone lying there.'

'Somebody saw him.'

The inspector's words reverberated like a judge's hammer. James glanced at Ted, who blanched. Was the policeman implying that somebody had seen everything that had happened last night, heard them scheming, too? Had the policeman's questions been mere preliminaries? Perhaps he had been playing a game with them, lulling them into a false sense of security before a final, devastating revelation which would expose their evasions?

'You're saying somebody actually saw what happened?' James could detect a tremor in his own voice, hoped it wasn't too obvious.

'Not for sure. I'm saying that somebody reported he was lying there injured. We were able to trace the call to Dave Hickson's own mobile phone but it wasn't anywhere in that yard, so it's unlikely he used it, especially in his state.'

Recovering his composure, Ted said, 'The mugger must have taken it.'

Davis eyed him. 'That mugger again. You have a one-track mind, son. I told you he still had his wallet with plenty of money in it, didn't I?'

James was pleased to see that Ted held the policeman's gaze and had the sense to shut up.

'It would be strange to beat a man so badly, then ring for an ambulance,' Davis continued, as though speaking thoughts outright as they entered his head, more to satisfy himself than the students, apparently. 'Not outside the bounds of possibility, I suppose, but most unusual.'

Neither student spoke. James wondered where Davis was going with this. If he suspected them why didn't he come out with it? Instead, he seemed to be dancing around them, falling short of any direct accusation. Or was that just his own guilt making him paranoid? Maybe this was the policeman's working habit, posing questions, thinking aloud, no ulterior purpose really but very irritating to his audience. The strain was making James feel sick but he fought it down, telling himself that nothing said so far incriminated them.

'Neither of you remembers anything unusual occurring last night? Nobody bothered your pal in the pub?'

Both students shook their heads. This was safer ground now, thank God.

'Dave Hickson had no enemies you know of, no recent arguments, anything in his life that would be a reason for someone to seek revenge in such a bloody way?'

'Nothing I can recall,' James answered. 'You, Ted?'

'No, nothing.' Ted paused. 'We belong to a student community, Inspector, so we've been pretty close-knit, really. Living and studying together, we'd probably have known if there was anything.'

Davis rubbed his chin thoughtfully, reached inside his pocket, handed his card to James. 'Well, as they always say, if you do think of anything …'

'Of course, Inspector,' James said. As he pocketed the card he felt a surge of relief. The ordeal was over now. The policeman had nothing worse to convey, no other questions for them which might trap them if they chose a wrong answer.

'Thanks for your co-operation,' Davis said, moving towards the door. 'You've been a big help.'

He paused with his hand on the handle of the kitchen door, then turned to face them again.

'One thing is making me curious.'

A gust of wind rattled the kitchen window. James felt his heart flutter but he forced himself to laugh.

'Don't worry, all students' flats pong a bit, Inspector. It's not a dead body in the pantry, if that's what you're puzzled about.'

Davis grinned but there was no mirth in his eyes.

'I'm familiar with the smell of a dead body, son. It was just that you never enquired how much memory your friend has retained. A lawyer needs all his faculties, doesn't he – needs to stay sharp?'

James reddened. 'I assumed he was going to be OK or you would have said otherwise.'

'Likewise,' Ted mumbled.

Davis nodded. 'Just a policeman's curiosity,' he remarked as he opened the door. 'It's unusual to meet lawyers who don't ferret out all the facts, as you remarked earlier.'

James forced a grin. Just when he'd regained confidence, the Inspector had fired a sarcastic shot across his bow again. It was a reminder to be careful.

'We're still in the embryonic stage, Inspector. Wait till we're fully fledged. But seriously, how bad is it?'

'He can remember most things but nothing about last night except that he was in a pub with you two.'

With that, Davis turned and walked into the hall. James followed him out and opened the front door for him. On the threshold, the policeman tucked his briefcase under his arm and faced James.

'We've managed to contact the lad's parents, by the way. They're coming up from Leeds to see him.'

'We'll visit later today,' James stated.

Halfway down the path Davis turned again. He had that same perplexed look on his face which James had begun to recognize as the preliminary to an awkward question. He groaned inwardly and prepared his guard.

'Forgot to tell you about the ecstasy tablets they found in the alley. Wouldn't connect to your friend, would they?'

James shook his head, stared at Davis. 'Never saw him with any.'

'Didn't think so,' said the inspector, and waved a hand in the air as he opened the gate.

James watched him go, sighed with relief and closed the door. When he returned to the kitchen he found Ted pacing the floor. His friend turned to face him, a hunted look on his face.

'I think he suspects us. The way he was asking those questions, it looked that way.'

'Just playing at Poirot,' James countered. 'We're both paranoid, aren't we? If they had anything concrete he'd have said so. They have to go into everything, you know that.'

That seemed to calm Ted. He stopped pacing, sat down and folded his arms.

'There was a moment when I considered telling him everything,' he suddenly announced. 'Maybe I – we – should have.'

James glared at him. 'It's gone too far for that and you know it. Don't worry, man, that's probably as bad as it will get as long as we hold our nerve.'

Ted sank into a chair. With his dishevelled hair, the bags under his eyes from a sleepless night, his face lined with worry, he seemed to have aged overnight. James felt a surge of sympathy for his friend.

'At the door he told me they'd found the tablets, asked me if they could be connected with Dave. I told him no, of course.'

Ted sighed. 'I've been sitting here thinking about Dave. Do you think he was into something we don't know about? He's a secretive sod, you know, different from us. I think he meant every word the other day in the coffee bar. Money is his god, so it wouldn't surprise me if he was into something heavy.'

The same thoughts had crossed James's mind. Hickson had always stressed that he came from a very different world from theirs, a fact he took every opportunity to harp on about. Had this episode been the result of a foray into that world, the one he said they've never understand? Until now James had considered his outpourings to be no more than the result of a chip on his shoulder, not to be taken too seriously. Maybe he hadn't recognized the true depth of his flatmate's attachment to the murkier side. If that was true, and he couldn't be certain it was, it was just possible that Hickson had been the architect of his own fate last night.

'Eases our consciences if he was playing with the big boys, doesn't it? Diverts attention away from us if they find anything untoward about Dave.'

Ted gave it some thought. 'I suppose so. It's a bit disloyal, a bit Machiavellian on our part to be thinking that, but we did save him from a worse beating, didn't we?'

'Of course we did!' James was happy to see his friend taking a more positive outlook than he'd shown so far. 'Anyway, our story is waterproof and it doesn't look like the guy we hit with the bricks has turned up dead, or that Inspector would have known about it, would probably have relished telling us about it.'

'God, will we ever be able to put this behind us?' Ted exclaimed.

As though the heavens had heard his plea, there was a sudden pitter-patter against the window and they both turned their heads. At last the clouds had released their burden. Gusts of wind hurled the rain on to the glass panes in angry flurries and it seemed to those inside that the elements themselves seemed to be conspiring to answer Ted's question, attacking the house in a display of their displeasure. This had been home for the last three years, but after the policeman's visit it suddenly seemed no longer a cosy haven full of the joys of youth.

11

A NURSE INTRODUCED James and Ted to Dave Hickson's parents, who were standing outside the single ward where he was recuperating. They were just about to leave for the guest house where they intended spending the night. The father was a small man with a pinched face and the mother was so much like her husband they could have been taken for blood relatives. James was struck by how inoffensive they looked, nothing of Dave's brashness apparent in either of them.

'They say he'll be all right,' the mother said, wiping a tear from her eye.

'But he's in a mess,' her husband added. 'I hope the police catch the bastard who did it. Not that I have much faith in the police. And if they do catch him the courts won't do much to him, will they?'

'We thought Dave's girlfriend would have been here by now,' the mother said. 'I was hoping to meet her. Our Dave could do with a little tender loving care, couldn't he? Do you lads know her?'

James and Ted exchanged glances, shook their heads in unison. Hickson hadn't had a steady girlfriend in the three years they'd known him. Had he been creating a fantasy of his life at university when he went home in the vacations or, which seemed most unlikely, somehow hiding this girl from his pals?

The mother frowned. 'We don't even know her name. He just

mentioned he had a lass and that she was a bit of a toff. Bit shy about it, I suppose.'

Her husband snorted. 'Our Dave, shy? You don't know what you're saying, lass. These lads will know him better. Bit secretive, maybe, but not shy in coming forward, not him.'

'We certainly hadn't a clue he was courting,' James said.

They spoke for a few minutes longer then, with James and Ted promising to keep an eye on their son's welfare, Hickson's parents set off for their guest house.

Even though they had been prepared for it, when they entered the ward it was a shock to see Hickson. His cheekbones were purple and puffed up, his eyes reduced to mere slits so that they weren't sure whether they were closed or not.

He must have had them open because a slurred voice said, 'Hello fellers. What do you think of my new digs? Three good meals a day and nurses appear at the touch of a button fighting over who should serve me. Beats the dingy flat and you two for company on a long, lonely night, eh!'

It was quite a long speech and in character, so it was a relief to both the visitors. Obviously Hickson must be feeling better than he looked. More cheering still, unless he was dissembling, his banter suggested he'd no idea how they'd conspired to leave him in that yard.

As they lowered themselves into the chairs next to the bed, James riposted in similar, light-hearted manner. 'Even if you've temporarily lost your looks, you certainly haven't lost your imagination, Hicko.'

Ted, more perfunctory, cut to the chase. 'How much do you remember, Dave? They told us not much.'

Hickson frowned. 'I remember being in the Blacksmith's with you and everything really, up to the moment I stepped outside. Then it's a blank.'

'You don't know who did this to you?' James enquired.

'Haven't a clue. The police are making enquiries.'

There was a sudden silence. Hickson turned his head from one to the other, studying them with eyes like small raisins.

'What happened to you two after I went outside?'

His question hit home hard. James could tell Ted's discomfort matched his own. Another lie was needed, or a confession, and they'd agreed to prevaricate for now. Yet, deceiving somebody they'd lived with for three years and whom, in spite of the difference in their backgrounds, they considered a friend, didn't come easily.

James cleared his throat, took the initiative. 'You went out to the toilet and took so long we thought you'd just gone straight home.'

A bit too hastily, Ted added 'We'd had a skinful, must have missed you in that yard. You know how dark it is out there.'

'When an inspector came to the flat to inform us you'd been beaten up, we thought you were still in bed,' James continued. 'It was quite a shock to hear what had happened. We felt ... guilty.'

'You shouldn't. Not your fault,' Hickson said, shifting uncomfortably. 'You know, according to the police somebody had the brass neck to steal my mobile phone and use it to report I was lying in that yard in a bad way. Imagine leaving me there in that condition.' Hickson's voice grew angry. 'Suppose I was lucky that whoever it was bothered to make that call.'

James mumbled, 'Could have been your attacker used the phone. Might have had a conscience.'

'Even if it wasn't him,' Ted said, his face reddening, 'people don't like to get involved these days, do they?'

Hickson shifted position again, winced with pain. 'Not what they teach you at private school, eh! Responsible citizenship and all that. Must have been ex-comprehensive, whoever he was.'

James blenched and quickly changed the subject. 'On the

bright side the doctors say you're going to be all right. It'll take time to recover but miraculously there's no bones broken. Maybe you'll even remember who attacked you and why.'

Sounding suddenly weary, Hickson said, 'Just glad I got my exams out of the way before this happened.'

They could see his eyes were starting to close. Having been warned by a duty nurse to stay no more than ten minutes, they stood up to go.

'Rest now, mate. We'll be back,' Ted told him.

As they moved to the door, James waved a hand and tried for the same levity that had begun the visit. 'We won't take advantage of your incapacitation to investigate that girlfriend you've been hiding away from us, the one your mother mentioned. Must be some looker, eh, Ted!'

With an effort, Hickson lifted his head off the pillow and glared. 'There's no girlfriend,' he said, with heavy emphasis on each word.

Wishing he hadn't bothered, James frowned. 'Just joking, man. Take it easy, now.'

Uncomfortable with their subterfuge, they walked in silence down the long corridors to the hospital entrance. It was a relief to step out into the night air. After the overheated atmosphere inside the hospital, the coolness outside was refreshing. James breathed it in deeply, consoled himself with the fact that at least the visit was over, that one more obstacle on the road back to normality had been faced and overcome.

'We could have told him, you know,' Ted mused, as they crossed the car park. 'He'd have seen the sense in our keeping quiet, surely he would?'

James wasn't so sure, didn't answer. When they were in the car he rested his arms on the steering wheel. As he stared ahead into the night he felt suddenly tired, as though he'd just sat all his exams in one day and his brain was protesting overload.

'He made me feel so guilty, Ted.'

'Me too!'

'There's a chance he'll never remember.'

'But he might, and he could be very angry!'

James pondered before he spoke. 'If he does remember, he'll also know we drove the guy off to save him.'

'We'd have to tell him we ran to protect ourselves.'

James started the engine. 'Agreed. But right now he's better off not knowing. Means he doesn't have to lie to the police. We know what that's like, don't we?'

12

DAVE HICKSON LAY back reasonably pleased with his perform-
ances. He'd seen enough films where the protagonist suffered, or
simulated, memory loss, and figured he'd put on a good show of
faking it for the police, his parents and his flatmates. Not that
he'd had to fake physical pain, because each time he moved his
body would protest, reintroducing him to the memory of that
savage beating. He knew, of course, what the beating had been
about, but no way had he expected it. Winston had been as high
as one of his punters last night. Dave had never seen him like
that before and could only think he had been an arbitrary choice
as a target. He was worried now because there were sure to be
consequences. Winston couldn't leave it there; he'd have to save
face and that meant he'd be back, more venomous. It would be
no good telling the police that; it would just make it worse for
himself in the long run. They'd poke their noses in and might
discover the truth about his own little arrangements. Though he
was reluctant to take it, there was only one course of action open:
he'd have to try to appease Winston. With that thought in mind
he reached under the pillow for the mobile phone he'd borrowed
from his father to replace his own. It took him a moment to
gather his resolve, then, steeled by the knowledge that the action
he was about to take would help his own cause, he dialled.

When a voice answered he hesitated: then, controlling his
fear, said, 'This is Hickson. Is that you, Winston?'

There was silence, an ominous silence, until at last a voice he could just recognize as Winston's rasped at him.

'You got some neck, man, but I gonna break it.'

'Why'd you do me?' Hickson said, trying to keep his composure. 'You'd have got your money. You know you would.'

Winston made a noise which sounded as though it was meant to be a laugh but came out as a crone's cackle.

'I got pressure, is why. But now you got pressure – more pressure.'

Hickson sucked in some air. 'They interfered, man. It wasn't my doing. Let me be and I'll give you their names if you want.'

Silence descended again. Hickson dared to hope it meant he was being given consideration.

'I'll still want my money.'

Hickson saw the chink of light in his dark dungeon, rushed at it. 'Just give me a bit more time. You put me in hospital. Can't do anything here, can I? Be reasonable.'

There was silence at the other end while Hickson held his breath. Then Winston snarled, 'Give me the names and you get a month.'

The light expanded, enveloped Hickson, a balm to his troubles. He felt blessed. He was almost free.

'It's a deal.'

'Their names.'

As he gave Winston what he wanted, a shudder ran through Hickson because he knew what he was unleashing. He dismissed it, telling himself that, though James and Ted had seen off Winston, they'd been quite willing to leave him in that yard for their own protection. He'd been aware of everything that happened that night in the yard as he lay semiconscious, too far out of it to move. He was only repaying them in kind. After all, he might have died because of their hesitation, their scheming to save their own necks.

He put the phone back under the pillow, lay back again exhausted from the effort and tension of that call to Winston. It had been an unpleasant business shopping his flatmates, a last resort really, but it had served his interests, saved him from Winston's retaliation and gained him time to gather the funds to pay him off. His car would have to go and that would be a pain but he'd be working in the law soon and would be able recoup his losses.

As he drifted into sleep he was thinking how it was time to give up the dealing. He wouldn't miss it, had only been in the low-down ranks anyway, selling enough to finance his time at university and to keep up with his flatmates who didn't know what it was like to struggle for money. It was a pity it had to end like this but, as James and Ted were about to find out, in the dog-eat-dog world he had moved in, every action had a reaction and better it was on their heads than his.

13

WINSTON PUT THE phone down, cursed the fact that Bradley's visit to his flat had coincided with the call from Hickson so that his cousin heard every word. He adjusted the bandage around his head, thinking he'd been lucky the damage hadn't been worse. It was his pride that was really hurting because, panicked by the amount of blood pouring down his face and head, he'd rung his cousin for help. Bradley had picked him up in his car himself, taken him to a private doctor for treatment. For that, Winston was grateful enough, but he was feeling the shame of it now, knowing that in Bradley's eyes he must be a total failure. In fact his cousin was probably wondering whether, family or not, it was worth keeping him on the payroll. If only he could save face.

'Now I know who did me,' he said, in response to his cousin's raised eyebrow. 'So I'll be taking care of them.'

Doleful eyes stared at him, as though they doubted he could be trusted to look after a baby sleeping in its cot. Embarrassed, Winston allowed his own eyes to wander around the room to avoid direct contact.

'So who are they?' Bradley enquired. 'These big tough guys.'

Winston hesitated, then said in a scarcely audible voice. 'Students, I think. Jus' students.'

Bradley walked to the window, stared out, said nothing. But

his silence seemed to speak volumes. Winston figured he was considering what to do with him; he expected he'd just blown his last chance. Yet he couldn't find it in his heart to plead, to add to the shame already whipping his manhood like a woman's scornful tongue.

When Bradley turned back to the room he looked thoughtful. 'So it was students,' he said. 'Well, we all students. Look at me, bro'. I'm a student of life, see. I know what make people what they be.'

Unable to understand what his cousin was leading to, pleased that he wasn't the recipient of his anger, Winston regained a little bravado.

'I'll do them, man. They'll never know what hit them.'

Bradley shot him a disdainful look. 'Sometimes you got to get physical, bro'. Other times you got to play. I think I use these students for bit play.'

Winston was bemused. 'Look what they did to me, man. I need to give them some back.'

His cousin shook his head. 'I have other plans for you.'

Winston didn't like the sound of that, started to worry. Other plans! That sounded ominous. What did it mean? It had the ring of redundancy to it, didn't it? Was his cousin going to declare he'd decided he didn't have what it takes?

'Other plans?'

Bradley levelled his gaze at him. Even so, Winston could see, from the distracted look in his eye, that part of his brain was elsewhere. The look scared him because he thought, not for the first time, that he saw madness in it, the madness of a man for whom, once he'd set on a course, there were no boundaries he wouldn't cross to reach his destination.

'I'm going to put you in a coffin,' he said, eventually.

Seeing the look of horror on Winston's face, he roared with laughter.

'But don't worry man, you going to be resurrected. You'll live through it.'

14

IT WAS SIX in the evening, day three after the events that had erupted into the students' comfortable lives with the suddenness of a flash flood. Not bothering to cook that night, they were sitting in a café in part of the town where back streets and alleys still predominated.

James bit into his parmo, a local delicacy he'd come to enjoy, studied Ted tucking into his beans on toast, and reflected that his friend's appetite, like his own, seemed to be returning at last. They had heard no more from the policeman and they'd read nothing in the papers. No news was good news. He considered the critical hour had probably passed; hopefully from now on they could relax a little, let their nerves recover. Dave, whom they'd visited that afternoon, seemed much better. His memory of the events of that fateful night had not improved, though in other respects his memory was fine. James supposed the blanks could be considered to be in their interests. In time they'd be able to banish the episode to the distant parts of their own brains, where it would no doubt remain as a scar on the landscapes of their lives, but with its power to disturb much diminished.

'So Dave's recovering,' Ted said, voicing parallel thoughts as he wiped vestigial tomato sauce from his mouth, 'and he's got all his faculties. So, apart from no memory of the assault itself, he's OK.'

James mused, 'The police must have hit a dead end, maybe put it on the back burner.'

He watched as a slow smile dimpled his friend's cheeks, his first since the night in the pub.

'So you can find something funny in all this, Ted?'

Putting on a more sober face, Ted replied, 'Sorry, it's just when you said "dead end".'

James's brow furrowed. 'So?'

Ted blushed. 'Just what we don't want, isn't it, a dead end? Don't want that fellow's body turning up, which is unlikely now, I'd say.'

James couldn't find much mirth there, surmised his friend's rather macabre reaction was more to do with finding an outlet for nervous tension. It had been building up inside both of them, stretching their mental resources to breaking-point. Still, it was a sign Ted was on the mend.

He looked at his watch. 'Let's head home,' he said, with a wry smile, 'before you split my sides with your wit.'

They walked out of the café feeling more cheerful than at any time in the last three days and turned into the warren of narrow, cobbled back lanes which would give them a short cut home. Halfway along they heard an engine roaring, saw a black van turn into the lane. James felt a sudden, grim presentiment, one that he couldn't explain, that something was not right here. His foreboding grew as the van advanced down the lane, which was hardly wide enough to accommodate it.

He heard Ted say, as though from a distance, 'What's that idiot doing?'

As he spoke, the vehicle accelerated, came straight at them, scattering empty dustbins that blocked its way. With screeching brakes it halted a yard away. Taken by surprise, they froze as the doors opened and three black men wearing bobble hats squeezed their way out. One of them produced a gun. He brandished it in their direction.

'In the van,' the armed man said. 'Move it!'

Stupefied, neither of them could move. It was as though they'd stepped out of their normal world on to a film set, crossed over the boundaries between reality and fiction. This couldn't possibly be happening to them, could it? Yet, that gun was real enough, as were the men built like refugees from a rugby scrum, who were now flanking them.

James realized they couldn't escape. They were trapped and helpless in the deserted lane. Before they knew it, the men were pushing them towards the van. Terrified of what might lie ahead, he thought about taking a chance, fighting back, but the gun and the implacable demeanour of the men discouraged him. There was an aura of wildness about them which left no doubt that they were capable of administering extreme violence without the faintest compunction.

One of the men bundled them into the back of the van and climbed in beside them. It was dark and they sat with their knees bunched up. The man sitting opposite them was holding a gun loosely, as though it was just another tool to him, one he was used to handling so that it had lost any mystique it might once have held with its power to administer death in the blink of an eye. Personal hygiene didn't count much with him either, because the odour of sweat and garlic emanating from him was nauseating.

James could feel Ted's body trembling. As though in empathy, his own hands started to shake. With an effort he controlled them, swallowed hard and tried to find his voice. He heard it emerge hoarse and desiccated as though a stranger's voice had usurped his own.

'What's happening, here? We've done nothing to you.'

Nobody answered him. The van suddenly shot backwards

over the cobbles so that they fell against one another. It backed on to the street, then accelerated forward. The buildings, the people on the streets, the passing vehicles were like something from another world, a safe, secure world they had left behind in that back lane and which bore no relationship to the nightmare unfolding before their eyes.

At last the driver spoke. 'The man wants to see you and the man gets what he wants.'

'Hear you boys like to play it rough,' the malodorous one added with a smirk. 'Well, it jus' got you promotion to the premier league.'

'There's been a mistake,' James whined, but a dark thought, which he fought against because of its terrifying implications, started to force its way forward in his mind.

The driver laughed, said to his companions, 'Maybe they thought they could make it into Europe, like Boro' team did – once.'

Ted found his voice but it was a rapid-fire, high-pitched screech. 'What are you talking about? Why are you doing this? Where are you taking us?'

The driver slapped the steering wheel with the palm of his hand and roared with laughter.

'Three questions from my boy there. They be going for the triple now.'

'They be hoping it not relegation,' the one in the passenger seat added, lowering his voice ominously.

James realized the uselessness of talking to the men. He thought it likely they were high on drugs. He caught Ted's eye, shook his head to indicate the futility of questioning them because their captors were just enjoying themselves at their expense. That dark thought was still in his head. What could 'playing rough' possibly refer to other than the confrontation in the yard? No matter how much he didn't want to admit it, there was more than a possibility that this was connected to the other night. They'd said the man wanted to see them. Could the man be the one they'd beaten? Was he seeking revenge for what they'd done to him? Those thoughts filled him with dread and he wondered if Ted was thinking on the same lines.

When they reached the outskirts of the town they were given black masks, told to put them on. Obviously, they were not to know where they were going. That gave James a morsel of hope to cling to because it suggested they would eventually be freed, otherwise why bother hiding anything?

Eventually the van stopped and they were hauled out. Disorientated, they bumped into each other and almost lost balance, which caused their captors more inane amusement. James couldn't hear any traffic, hardly any noise at all in fact, except for a chorus of birdsong, its sweetness incongruent with his desperate mood. He figured they must be somewhere in the country. Someone took his arm and pulled him along. He heard a door open and close behind him and was conscious of a musty, damp smell, redolent of an old building. Again he was pushed forward, then, when he came to a stop, his mask was removed.

They were in a long hall devoid of carpeting, furniture or ornament. A black man with bulked-up muscles and a shaven head which served to emphasize a mangled ear stood a few feet away. He raised an eyebrow and the scar above it puckered as he looked them up and down like a sergeant-major giving new recruits the once over, the scornful twist to his lip conveying that he couldn't believe they had the temerity to enrol for battle.

Glancing over their heads at his men, he commented, 'Just little boys in short pants. Their mamas not know they're out.'

The men behind them sniggered. James felt his hackles rise. The humiliation made him want to fight back, helped him find his voice.

'I think there's been a mistake.'

The man stepped forward, brought his arm up as though about to strike and James flinched in expectation. But instead of a blow, calloused fingers caressed his cheek. His stomach turned at the intrusive intimacy.

'Lily-white skin,' the man said. 'Pure, lily-white skin.' He withdrew his fingers, stared at the students. 'Two white swans gliding along, all innocence. But their souls not pure.'

Ted spoke at last, his voice quivering. 'What … are you talking about?'

'Life and death is what I talk about. You on trial here, boys. I'm the judge, see. You fellers be lawyers. You know all about trials and judges.'

James glanced at Ted. Was he thinking the same as he was, that this must have to do with the other night? Yet, if that was the case, how on earth had these men found them? It didn't seem likely that the man they'd beaten had had a clue who they were. It had been so dark there in the yard. And surely he would be here now if this was about revenge. Eventually he had to ask:

'Is this anything to do with what happened in—'

'Happened! Happened!' the man yelled, drowning his voice. The veneer of calm had vanished in an instant. He pushed them both in the chest and they fell back against his henchmen.

'That what you call it, a happening? Let's have a trial 'bout a happening. Like it was just a tea party or somethin' with your posh friends. That what they teach you, uh?'

Neither student answered him because there was a look in his eyes beyond the normal. They feared saying the wrong thing, provoking the demon caged inside him which seemed ready to unleash itself at any moment. A silence descended in the hall, a silence charged with a tension so palpable that James felt as though the old walls were about to implode. Then, at last, the demon retreated, and the man's eyes regained a semblance of normality. He swiped the air with his hand and turned his back.

'Bring them lily-whites,' he said and disappeared into a room off to his left.

James stumbled into the room first. His eyes took a moment to adjust because the curtains were closed and it was poorly lit by candles placed at intervals. But there was enough light for him to see that the room was as sparsely furnished as the hall: no carpet, no furniture, it was more or less a shell. The man had taken a position in the middle, arms folded like an imperious warlord about to exercise his right over life and death. The machete he held in his right hand added to that aura. Beyond the man, partially hidden by his bulk, he noticed a long box sitting on a table, surrounded by small candles on the floor beside it. The black curtains hanging on the window were like funeral drapes. What on earth was going on? Just for a moment James thought he had the answer. This was surely a set-up, an ill-judged stunt organized by their fellow students as an end of term prank. Maybe these gangsters were actors hired to bring them here. Just a crazy stunt! There were those amongst their fellow students who were far out enough to arrange it.

The big man unfolded his arms, stepped to the side so that he no longer obstructed their view of the box. He pointed the machete, first in the direction of the box, then at them.

'Take a look!'

'This has gone far enough,' James pronounced. 'Whoever set this up needs treatment.'

His answer was a swipe from behind which sent him hurtling forward. Given similar encouragement, Ted followed him.

'Take a look, like you told,' the man snarled, his lip curling as he ran his fingers along the blade.

Shoulder to shoulder, like priests in awe of a sanctified relic, they edged forward, peered inside. James felt his stomach muscles pull so tight they seemed about to tear apart. He heard Ted gasp. A body lay in the makeshift coffin, dressed in a long white robe, a bandage around the top of the head. James's hope that this was a stunt immediately disintegrated. Though it had been dark when they'd tangled with him, the face of the black man they'd encountered in the back yard of the Blacksmith's Arms was burned into their brains and there was no doubt it was the same man lying there, the nemesis that had haunted the last few days and nights.

Ted groaned, 'My God, he's dead.'

Strong hands pulled them away. The man stepped close to them, raised his machete. His lower lip curled again like a spoiled child's when it has been denied.

'Bad enough you interfered with business,' he snarled, 'but that man lying cold and stiff be my cousin.'

The students reeled backwards. Ted gripped James's arm, his fingers digging into his flesh like a drowning man's before the sea overwhelms him. Transfixed, they focused on the raised machete.

The man held his threatening pose, a crazy frenzy in his eyes. Then, as though the storm inside him had blown itself out, he shook his head and lowered the weapon. The students felt a surge of relief, but the terror remained. This reprieve was likely to be temporary. Their worst fears had been confirmed when they'd looked into that coffin. For sure, this man had every reason to kill them and was mad enough to do it.

Fingering his mangled ear with his free hand, the man said, 'Maybe I let you off. I think about it. I see you just babies, not professionals.'

'We didn't mean to kill him,' Ted pleaded.

A quiver in his voice, James chimed in, 'We're so sorry.'

71

The man glanced at the coffin. A moment ago he'd been as vicious as a wild animal about to attack. Now he seemed more sombre than anything.

'My cousin was a weak man,' he said, turning back to them. 'Even though he was my blood, maybe I give you way out. What you say 'bout that?'

'We'd take it,' Ted said, without hesitation. 'Just give us a chance.'

James was bemused but figured that if there was an opportunity to extricate themselves, they had to pursue it.

'We'd do anything. Just let us go.'

The man stroked his chin as he gave it consideration. Time stretched, teasing their emotions as they waited.

At last he said, 'Killing him cost me business. You help me with business, we be even. I even forget my cousin lying there cold as stone because of two lily-whites.'

James drew in a breath. 'What do we have to do?'

The man stooped, placed the machete on the floor, straightened again and headed for the door, calling for his underlings to follow him and bring the students too. They were herded into the kitchen. Except for a table and chairs, it was as bare as the front room. James and Ted were bundled into the chairs and the man sat down opposite them.

'I give you holiday,' he announced. 'In beautiful Trinidad. All expenses paid.'

James glanced at Ted. He looked as perplexed as he was himself. In short time, the man before them had changed from a furious vigilante, the avenger of his dead cousin, to a much cooler customer, more like a slippery time-share purveyor with a hidden agenda. James had little doubt that the agenda would involve something illegal, but he was prepared to agree to anything which would help them escape from this crazy man who had menaced them with the machete. Perhaps they could renege later but right now agreeing to anything that would keep them breathing was the only option. Ted would surely think the same.

'We agree – but there are no free rides, are there?' James said, in a resigned tone.

More blunt, Ted said, 'What's the catch?'

For the first time the man smiled. He shook his head. 'Can tell you boys is lawyers, always look for percentage. Well, I tell you the truth. I bring two girls out of Trinny. If they come with two boys, it look cool. Without a male, they noticed more.'

James understood what he wasn't saying. Ted, he was sure, must have grasped the subtext but he voiced it anyway.

'He wants us to smuggle drugs.'

Before Ted could answer, the man came back at James. 'Not you. The girls will carry. There be no risk to you. You there for the ride.'

James pondered it. 'What if they're searched, these girls?'

'No worries, man. You just met them. Worst happens, you ain't carrying.'

Ted said, 'After that, it's over? You'll let it go?'

'Man of my word. You do it, I let you be, forget you murder my cousin. I bury his body where no one finds it. If you don't, you dead meat.'

James didn't see much choice. He was sure this man was perfectly capable of carrying out his threat. The only way out was to agree to anything. Later, they might think of a way to avoid carrying out his instructions, though quite how, he had no idea. Glancing at Ted, he saw his friend stare into space as though already foreseeing doom waiting somewhere out there in the ether. He spoke up for both of them.

'We have no choice. We'll do what you say.'

The man grinned, stretched his massive frame. 'We know

where you live, be in touch soon. Have your passports ready. Five days in Trinny will be a breeze.'

At a signal from their boss his henchmen hauled them to their feet and escorted them down the hall, the man following on behind. Before they stepped out of the front door one of the men put the blindfolds back on.

'Don't think about police,' the man said. 'You do, they be told how you is my cousin's murderers. Betray me, you dead anyway.'

None of the escorts spoke on the ride back. The CD player blasted out a succession of reggae tunes and rap which would have made speaking difficult. Their masks were removed when they hit a built-up area. In the near distance, James could see the Cleveland Hills, Roseberry Topping lording it over them. The familiarity of the scenery, knowing they were near home, gave him a measure of relief but it was tempered by the pressure they were still under.

The driver pulled into the street where they lived, stopped the car a few doors up. The malodorous one pointed to the house.

'Go home to mummy,' he said. 'Tell her you been out playing with bad boys.'

They got out of the car and as soon as their feet touched the pavement it shot off. In seconds, it was out of sight. They stared after it, then at each other, their relief at being alive mingling with trepidation because though they had crested one wave another was gathering force, ready to sweep into their lives and carry them who knew where.

James put a comforting arm round his friend's shoulder, guided him towards the flat.

'My God,' Ted groaned, tears rushing into his eyes. 'What are we going to do now? I never thought—'

James, close to tears himself, cut in, 'We'll have to do it. I don't fancy ending up on the bottom of the River Tees.'

As James put his key in the lock, Ted grabbed his arm, a desperate look in his eyes.

'We should have told the police. We still can. They'll protect us.'

James shook him off, said nothing. He waited until they were inside and collapsed into the chairs in the living room, mentally exhausted from the ordeal.

'Think about it. It's too late now for the police.'

Ted looked confused, like a little boy lost at a crossroads, unsure which direction to take.

'They might understand,' he muttered after a long pause. 'We could say we ran away because we panicked.'

James shook his head. 'We're law students, remember. People will say we should have had the intelligence to know better. Whatever, we'd be punished and our careers, our future status in life, would be down the pan.'

'Our families,' Ted moaned. 'They'd be ashamed.'

'We could end up in prison. That dog-eared cretin will have contacts in prison. He said he'd make sure we suffered if we talked.' James hesitated, reluctant to say it, 'I'm afraid we'd be better taking our chances in Trinidad. We won't actually be carrying drugs and it gives us a chance to get out of this mess without any consequences.'

Ted mumbled unenthusiastically, 'I suppose as long as we don't have to carry drugs not much can go wrong.'

'Let's sleep on it, if we can sleep. We'll see if we're of the same mind in the morning.'

As he got into bed the conversation with Hickson after Deadman's lecture came into James's mind. He recalled him saying that people would do anything to preserve their status, their way of life. He and Ted had disputed that idea and Hickson had told them, in that superior way of his, that they didn't know anything. Now it seemed the conversation had been almost prophetic. They had a difficult choice to make and it looked as though Hickson had been on the mark; self-interest had to prevail or their lives would be irrevocably damaged.

15

NEXT MORNING, MOST inopportunely, Liz visited the flat early. With so much on their minds, visitors were the last thing James and Ted wanted. Forcing himself to act normally, James made her a cup of coffee but, no matter how she tried to fill in the lulls, the conversation was stilted, as though they were people meeting for the first time rather than close friends.

'I've been to see Dave,' she said, eventually.

'We saw him yesterday,' Ted muttered.

She sipped at her coffee. 'He seemed fine.'

James glanced at Ted. 'We're sure he's going to be OK.'

A long silence followed. James knew she must sense something was wrong. She was having to force conversation; he and Ted were finding it difficult to concentrate on anything. At last she voiced her suspicions.

'Is there something wrong here? I feel like I'd be better talking to the walls. Have I offended the legal eagles in some way?'

'I'm OK,' Ted said, too abruptly.

'James?' she queried. 'Have I ruffled your feathers?'

James gave her a weak smile. 'It's just that I'm feeling a bit off. Would you mind if I went back to bed? Think it's something I've eaten.'

'Please do,' she told him. 'I'll bet it's the post-exam celebrations catching up on you at last!'

He didn't answer, just rose and headed for the door, his shoulders sagging so that he was more like an old man than his usual vibrant self.

Almost as an afterthought, he called out, 'Sorry! See you later.'

Ted remained where he was. He stared at the clock on the mantelpiece as though willing himself to another time, another place, as though he was unaware of Liz sitting opposite him. The sound of the clock ticking filled the silence between them like a heart beating.

Liz shifted in her chair. 'You're making me feel miserable, cousin. Please tell me what's going on. There's something. I know there is.'

He turned to her with a haunted look in his eyes, as though a devil was possessing him, draining his vitality. It seemed to take an effort for him to concentrate.

Suddenly, in an angry voice, he said. 'Are you worried, Liz?'

She frowned, puzzled by his manner and tone. 'Worried?'

'You're not really a nice person, are you – cousin?' he snapped, more viciously than she believed possible of him.

She visibly reeled. This wasn't the quiet, polite Ted she knew. What had got into him? Then a thought struck her, making her go red. Had he found out about her and Hickson?

'What have I done to merit this?'

He sneered, his voice rising. 'You're betraying James with Hickson, aren't you?'

Liz glanced towards the door, hoping James wouldn't hear and come to investigate. Ted shot her a contemptuous look.

'Don't worry. I'm not going to tell him. It'd hurt him too much and right now he's got other things to think about.'

'How did you know?' she whispered.

'I've got eyes even if he hasn't. Besides, I came home for something I'd forgotten about a month ago and heard you in the bedroom with him.'

Flustered by this turn of events, Liz stood up and made for the door. Not even looking at her, Ted put his head in his hands and stared at the carpet. At the door she hesitated, then turned back to him. He wasn't even looking at her, as though he'd already dismissed her from his mind.

'I know I've got to choose,' she said. 'Just give me a little time.'

She thought he wasn't going to answer. Then, suddenly, in a faraway voice, he said, 'I won't tell him if that's what's worrying you. That's your job. We might be going away for a few days, James and I – just a change. That'll give you time to think – if you need it.'

She took a deep breath and said, 'Thanks. I will do some serious thinking, I promise. I knew it couldn't go on. It had to come to this.'

'Sooner the better then,' Ted called after her as she left the room.

16

JAMES STARED OUT of the window, trying to come to terms with everything. He felt like a stranger who had stumbled into someone else's world. He would have given anything to be back in England, his old, happy self once again. He focused on the dreamscape not more than fifty yards away, the blue sea rolling on to the palm-fringed white sand where, for the last three days, he and Ted had lain in the sun in a semi-drunken stupor, endeavouring to escape their apprehension. Another time, other circumstances, he'd have been in his element. Trinidad, with its carnival atmosphere and happy people, was a beautiful place to relax. But its charms couldn't banish the foreboding. He felt like a soldier waiting to go into battle, hoping the dreaded moment wouldn't come, knowing in his soul it would inevitably arrive, the outcome uncertain, survival dependent on his own nerve or another's whim. And it had all happened so quickly. They'd been swept up like the driftwood lying on that white sand and had been carried along by the speed of events. Within days of their kidnap travel itineraries, tickets and instructions had arrived through their letterbox. Unable to see any viable alternative, they'd gone with the current and been cast up here to await their fate.

He turned back to the room in time to see Ted, who was lying on the bed, take a long swig from a bottle of rum. Aware of James's displeasure, he corked the bottle.

'No more of that now,' James told him. 'We have to be totally sober when we go to that airport, have to look perfectly natural, not draw attention in any way.'

Ted glanced at the bedside clock. In a resigned voice he said, 'Another few hours and we'll be on that plane.'

'Tonight we'll sleep in our own beds, forget about all this, be able to get on with our lives.' James did his best to sound optimistic but there was a hollowness in his voice. 'So keep your chin up.'

'I'm cool man,' Ted grunted.

A faraway look in his eye, he looked beyond James at the blue sky before bringing his gaze back to his friend.

'From paradise lost to paradise regained, eh? Easy as that! Just one little flight in the big blue is all it takes.'

James said quietly, 'Let's just keep in mind, if it all goes belly-up, that we're not the ones carrying the stuff.'

'Sounds foolproof,' Ted said, throwing his legs off the bed and pulling on his shirt. 'Innocents abroad, us.'

'You've got it. So let's get packed. We have to meet the girls at the airport in two hours.'

Ted shook his head as though he couldn't quite believe it. 'Our blind dates with destiny.'

He pulled on his shorts, wandered to the window and stood beside his friend. 'Strange, isn't it,' he commented, 'how they've just left us alone while we've been here. No contact at all.'

'Suppose they think the less we know about them and their business the better – but I bet they've been watching us,' James picked up a sheet of paper. 'These instructions are clear enough. A guy called Cameron will meet us in the airport coffee bar and introduce us to the girls.'

'Wonder what kind of girls carry drugs?' Ted mused.

James picked up his suitcase, threw it on the bed and started to pack.

'What kind do you think? Poor girls from the slums who are willing to risk anything for money. Girls who've hit bad times and think it will get them out. Gullible girls who believe what men tell them. Take your pick.' He sighed. 'But this is about us, not the girls. What they're like, what happens to them, is not our concern. Survival is our priority!'

The friends exchanged meaningful glances. What they were doing was so alien to them, they could hardly believe the shift in their moral compass.

Ted voiced his discomfort. 'What's happening to me? I really don't care about the girls as long as we come through safe and sound.'

'Me neither,' James confessed.

A silence settled on the room, then James said, 'Don't want to admit it, but Hickson was right when he said people will do anything if the stakes are high enough. We were the ones who were wrong about that.'

Ted picked up the bottle of rum, saw the look James gave him and put it down again. 'There's no justice, is there, James? Dave is lying cosy in that hospital bed right now while we suffer because we went to help him.'

James stroked the bristle on his chin. 'I think there was more going on in Dave's life than we know. That guy we killed was mixed up with a crazy bunch. Was it just by chance he attacked Dave in a back alley? How did they get on to us so quickly?'

'We'll find out,' Ted said, his jaw resolute. 'When we get back, we'll find out. We'll challenge him.'

They finished packing, then went down to breakfast. Knowing what the day held for them, neither could stomach food; they only managed black coffees. When they went to check out the girl at the desk said the bill was already paid and a taxi ordered for them. That wasn't a surprise because their instructions had informed them that it would all be taken care of. When the taxi arrived they handed over their luggage and climbed in.

During the journey the radio was tuned in to a station that played a constant stream of reggae songs. The driver knew them all and sang along to them as he drove. His singing and cheerful demeanour were irritants because it was all out of keeping with how they were feeling. With each passing mile, their tension was building and his carefree behaviour didn't help.

As they approached Piarco airport James decided to make an announcement.

'Listen, Ted, I know this is a bad time but this business has set me thinking I'd like a more settled life when we get back home, so I phoned Liz last night and asked her to get engaged.'

Ted swallowed. 'And was she agreeable?'

'She said she'd have a good think about it over the next few weeks. Apparently she'd been wondering if we should take our relationship on to another stage.'

'I'm happy for you, then. Can't say you chose a good moment to tell me, or to ask her, but I hope it works out for both of you.'

17

PIARCO AIRPORT BUSTLED with people. Given the heat, most were dressed in shorts, sandals and shirts. With typical flamboyance, many of the locals wore loud shirts that competed in garishness. James felt like a spectator watching other people's lives, each of which seemed to have a purpose whilst he seemed to have lost his. He realized that that sense of alienation arose from his purpose here, one that made him an outsider to the law he'd intended to serve as his chosen career. Now he was about to betray that same law. Ted nudged his elbow, broke into his unproductive thought pattern. His friend pointed to a sign that indicated the coffee bar and they lugged their cases through the throng.

Settling down in the coffee bar, they drank coffee while they waited for the man called Cameron. After half an hour he still hadn't shown and they were growing increasingly anxious. Ted annoyed James by constantly rapping on the table with his fingers and shuffling in his seat. Fighting his own nervousness, he tried not to let his annoyance show and sat motionless.

'Maybe they've decided against it,' Ted said, a little optimism creeping into his voice. 'Maybe we won't have to do it.'

James scowled. 'Pigs might fly. They've brought us all the way here, haven't they, so I doubt they'll back out.'

Minutes later a West Indian in a grey suit, white shirt and blue tie approached their table. Crinkly hair, grey at the temples, combined with his sartorial elegance to lend him the air of a distinguished businessman. Right until the moment he put his coffee down on their table and sat down, James didn't think he could be their contact. He'd been expecting someone much more rough and ready.

'The name's Cameron, fellers. You've been expecting me,' he said in a cultured voice. He folded his arms and flashed a smile which never reached his eyes but showed off a set of perfect white teeth. 'I take it you are ready?'

'We're as ready as we ever will be,' James told him. He could see a foxlike cunning in the man's eyes that hinted at another life, one far beyond the respectable businessman image he must have acquired somewhere along the line. James saw, in a flash, that this man possessed a feral street-wisdom forged in a life he couldn't begin to imagine.

'You understand everything you were told?' Cameron continued. 'You understand you're just there for the ride? Once you're through customs at Bristol you walk away from the girls. They know themselves what to do then. You got all that?'

'We just want it over and done,' Ted said, 'so let's get on with it.'

Introductions over and his appraisal of them finished, Cameron sat back and waved a hand towards a table at the far side of the coffee bar where two dark skinned girls were seated. At his signal they stood up and manoeuvred their way between the tables with their suitcases.

James pulled out an extra chair. Without acknowledgements for any of the men, the girls sat down. James guessed they were both in their early twenties and was surprised by how smart and sophisticated they appeared. Nothing about them suggested they were the type to be carrying drugs. But what was the type?

When the girls were seated Cameron said, 'Two more things

for you boys. Smile a little, to keep everything natural. More important, the girls can't eat with what's inside them, so help them out with the meals. That way the stewardesses won't see too much food left and be suspicious.'

'What if we're searched?' Ted said, then glanced sheepishly at the girls. 'I mean – what if the girls are searched?'

Cameron's cold eyes slanted towards Ted. 'You're playing the percentages here and they're in your favour, so be cool, man. The girls know the score. Besides, we've got people in customs working for us. They'll turn a blind eye.' He faced the girls, his tone bordering on the dismissive. 'Once you're through, you know what to do, right?'

Wide-eyed, like slaves in awe of a master, both girls nodded. James sensed that, under a veneer of control, the girls were as nervous as he was, their awareness of the risk they were about to take intensified now the stage lights were on and it was close to curtain-up. His own sense of imminence was heightened. How much worse must they be feeling with drugs inside them? He gave himself a mental ticking off. As he'd told Ted earlier, they could only afford to think of themselves if they were to get through this.

Cameron was looking at his watch. 'Check-in time,' he announced and pointed to James and the girl seated opposite him. 'You two go first, the other two a bit later. You stay together like boyfriend and girlfriend. But from now on you don't know the other pair. They're strangers, see, and you're oblivious.'

'We've got it,' James said.

Cameron's eyes roamed over the faces of his four charges in turn, making one last assessment of their preparedness. 'Stick to it and nothing is likely to happen. Otherwise ...' He didn't need to finish the sentence.

James steeled himself. He stood up and his allotted partner

rose with him. With a nod at Ted, meant to reassure him, he picked up his case and moved off, the girl following with her own case. As he walked away he could feel a sick sensation in his stomach, as though he'd just raised a pistol to his head in a mad game of Russian roulette and he was only one twitch of his trigger finger from blowing his whole world apart.

The sensation stayed with him, but checking in their cases, passing through passport control and customs went smoothly. The girl kept her nerve admirably, kept smiling at him as they walked past the uniformed officials. Once they were safely through, he tried to talk to her but her answers were monosyllabic and he got the message that she wasn't interested in conversation with him. In the concourse, where they waited for the call to board their flight, he noticed Ted and his partner but made no attempt to acknowledge him.

When their flight call came over the tannoy they queued with the other passengers and handed in their boarding-passes. Once they were inside the plane, a stewardess with a rigor mortis smile showed them to their seats. James ushered the girl into the seat nearest the window. When he saw Ted and his partner board and take seats near the front, he breathed a sigh of relief. A long flight lay ahead and they were far from home and dry, but at least the business was half done. He closed his eyes as the plane sped down the runway and prayed their luck would hold when they reached Bristol.

Once they were in the air he glanced at the girl. She didn't look so cool now. Tiny eruptions of sweat beads were gathering on her brow. Her body was too upright and her dark-brown eyes were staring ahead as though she was hypnotized. He figured a careful observer would know straight away that something was bothering her. That worried James but at the same time he felt a wave of sympathy for her. Beneath the smart clothes and sophisticated act, he saw she was little more than a vulnerable child, probably in her late teens. He handed her his handkerchief.

'Wipe your brow. Lean back. Look as though you're at peace with the world. It's going to be OK.'

She took the handkerchief, gave him a weak smile and whispered her thanks.

A stewardess announced that the in-flight movie was *Sliding Doors*, starring Gwyneth Paltrow. James, to divert his mind from worrying thoughts, tried to watch. He didn't succeed because the film was about how a decision, trivial and innocuous seeming at the time, could alter life dramatically. The irony wasn't lost on him and it made him feel worse. Had his own decision irrevocably altered the direction of his life? How many other people's lives would be affected by the drugs they were smuggling? James's conscience bothered him when he considered that bleak fact.

After the movie finished the meal was served. He ate his own and most of the girl's. The girl fell asleep and James closed his eyes, hoping he would be able to drift off himself, kill some more time.

A dig in the ribs woke him with a start. For a second, he wondered where he was. He heard the girl's voice in his ear.

'You were snoring, man. I worried everybody would hear you.'

He straightened up. 'How long have I been asleep?'

'Over an hour. I let you be 'til people stare.'

Suitably admonished, he glanced at his watch. He was surprised because it was six in the evening and they were due in at seven. God, he must have been more tired than he realized, the tension draining his resources.

Right at that moment he wished he could stop time, because soon he was going to have to face the long walk through customs. He thought about his parents, how it would affect them if he was caught. But there was no way out now. It was too late to go back. The die was already cast and what would be would be.

The plane began its descent. The initial bump as it hit the runway gave way to a steady deceleration. On past flights James had felt relieved when he was back on terra firma but this time was different; this time the heavens seemed a safer place for him than mother earth. When the plane came to a halt, he undid his seat belt and glanced at the girl's face. He was glad to see she looked composed.

They disembarked, got on to one of the buses designated to take them to the terminal. He spotted Ted on the same bus and their eyes met for a moment. He noticed a disturbing, haunted look in his friend's eyes which he hoped wouldn't be apparent to the customs officers. The bus dropped them at a building whose façade seemed cold and functional, like the exterior of a prison.

As he'd been told to do, he stuck close to the girl and showed his passport to the bored looking official, who flipped through the pages. The fellow scrutinized him with eyes which showed all the emotion of a lizard's. He tried to affect an air of insouciance but his stomach was churning. His passport was returned without comment and the girl's passport was given no more than a cursory glance. Their sense of relief was short-lived however, because they knew the real test of their nerves would come after they collected their bags and had to pass through customs.

'You did well,' he told the girl, forcing a calmness he didn't feel into his voice as they walked down a long corridor to the baggage collection. 'Keep it up. It won't be long till we're home free.'

He smiled as he said it, just a happy guy making a humorous comment to his girlfriend, but the smile froze on his lips when he spotted Ted up ahead. He knew instantly that something was badly wrong. The girl was leaning awkwardly on Ted, her handbag swinging loosely in the crook of her arm. She looked like a lame old woman. Either that, or drunk. It drew attention when they were meant to blend in with the crowd. He heard his own girl gasp when she noticed. His first instinct was to help his friend, but he realized that any move he made could draw more attention, make the situation worse.

'We have to walk past them,' he said, hating himself for it. 'It's too dangerous to stop and help.'

From the pained look on her face, he could see that she was going to find that difficult. For all James knew the other girl could be a friend or relative, so her emotions might get the better of her. He was terrified that she was going to lose control, blow it for them. But she kept going and they passed Ted and the girl without so much as a glance in their direction.

They soon entered the huge area designated for baggage collection. Luggage was already circling on the carousel. As they waited for their cases James kept searching the crowds for sign of his friend. Eventually he saw him. Ted had one arm around the girl. She was leaning on him for support and he looked as stiff as a soldier on parade. It was clear that something was wrong. Perhaps the girl was ill. James consoled himself with the thought that as long as she was on her feet they had a chance. With a bit of luck it would appear that the girl was indeed ill, or had been drinking excessively and her grim-looking boyfriend wasn't too impressed.

James's case appeared, the girl's a little way behind it. He dragged them off the carousel. The girl took hers and they set off for the customs channels. Before they entered James glanced over his shoulder. Ted wasn't too far behind, carrying two cases and supporting the girl.

Entering the 'nothing to declare' channel James was aware of uniformed officials watching. He forced himself to maintain the same pace. The channel seemed to go on for ever, and each time he put his foot down he expected to hear a voice calling out telling him to halt. His nerves exaggerated every sound. The girl's heavy breathing reverberated in his ear and he was conscious of his own rapid exhalations, of his heart thumping in his chest. Up ahead he could see green exit signs. Beyond the signs they would be safe. So near and yet so far. It made the temptation to increase his pace even greater and he had to rein himself in.

He risked a glance over his shoulder. Ted and the girl were halfway through. If anyone suspected anything, surely they would have been stopped by now. He faced forward again, daring to think they were going to make it. Just another few minutes and they'd be home and dry. Later, they'd celebrate surviving this nightmare. He wasn't a bad person, really. Neither was Ted. They'd never transgress again, either of them. This experience was enough for a lifetime.

His moment of optimism was terminated when he heard shouts from behind. They were like a dagger plunging into his back. The hairs on his neck bristled. He jerked to a halt as a wave of fearful anticipation coursed through his body and his thoughts spiralled to the last place he wanted them to go. He saw the girl's mouth draw back as they turned simultaneously. Other people were looking back with puzzled expressions. Through the crowd, he caught a glimpse of Ted down on his knees beside the girl who was lying flat out on the concrete. Three uniformed customs officers arrived on the scene and one bent down to cradle the girl's head. Another started talking into a radio. At that moment, Ted suddenly raised his head, looked through the crowd straight at James. His face wore the haunted expression of a man who has gambled and lost everything. James, lost in his own helplessness, knew he'd never forget that look as long as he lived.

He forced himself to snap out of it, gripped the girl's arm. She tried to pull away, wanting to go back to her friend. He held on, hauled her back, using all his strength to keep her close. He knew what she was feeling because he was feeling the same. But what good could they do? They would only endanger themselves.

'Don't be foolish,' he snapped and made her keep walking.

When they were through the exit and in the main concourse they put their cases down. The crowds swept past them. Disorientated and shocked, James wondered what he should do now. He was aware of a sense of relief that he was free, and he felt ashamed. How could he feel relief when his friend was back there? He glanced at the girl. Tears were streaming down her cheeks.

'What can we do?' she groaned, wringing her hands together in a way that he feared might draw attention.

He forced himself to focus. The instructions had been clear enough. Once through customs, they had to part from the girls, go their separate ways. The girls knew whom to contact and how. Right now, James wanted to be free of her so he could devote his thoughts to Ted.

'Do what they told you to do,' he said impatiently. 'You can't help your friend now.'

She met his gaze with a helpless, doe-eyed look. He regretted his tone but he knew that a ruthless indifference was more likely to get her moving. If she lingered she might do something silly. The sooner she was on her way out of there the better.

'Get going!' he admonished, 'or it'll be the worse for you with the men who put you up to this.'

His harshness had the desired effect. With a hurt look in her eyes she lifted her case and took a step away from him.

'What about you, man?' she said, in a voice just above a whisper. 'You going to walk away?'

'What the hell can I do?'

She didn't answer, just turned her back on him. He stood and watched until she disappeared into the crowds, then concentrated on his own situation. He was supposed to leave the airport alone, meet up with Ted in the long stay park where they'd left their car. Now the chances of his friend turning up were about zero. Customs would find drugs in the girl's stomach, wouldn't let Ted walk away. Yet he could hardly just head home, abandon his friend.

He found a seat, tried to figure out his next move. An hour later he made the decision to head back to the car, catch some sleep, maybe drive back home at first light. If by a miracle he was released Ted would probably head for the car anyway. With a heavy heart he headed out of the terminal and climbed on to a courtesy bus which took him to the car park.

Luckily he was the one with the car keys. He threw his case into the boot and settled into the driver's seat. As soon as he leaned back, he could feel his eyelids growing heavy. It wasn't long before he fell asleep.

18

THE DISTANT STACCATO rapping intruded from another world. Lost in a dream, he was only dimly aware, didn't want to know, just wanted to be left alone where he felt safe.

The rapping grew louder, raking his sleep like a machine gun now. He succumbed, opened his eyes reluctantly. For a moment he was disorientated. Then, as the rapping reached crescendo, the real world banished his dream and, remembering everything, he knew he was in the car. He turned his head towards the sound, reeled away from the face framed in the passenger window that was staring into his own with eyes bulging. Then he realized it was no stranger's face. It was Ted's face. But how could that be? Daring to hope the gods had been kind, that everything was going to be all right, he opened the door.

Without a word, Ted threw his case on to the back seat, sank into the passenger seat and let out a long sigh. A beam from a passing car's headlights lit up his face and James saw the strain etched into his features.

'Thank God I'm out of there,' he said. 'Thought I'd had it.'

James had so many questions he didn't know where to begin. He was finding it difficult to believe the evidence of his own eyes, that it really was Ted sitting there beside him in the flesh, not some ghostly figure conjured from his own tormented mind.

In his bemusement, he stated the obvious. 'They let you go!'

Ted nodded. 'In the end they bought the story that I was merely helping her with the suitcase after making her acquaintance at Piarco airport. I had to hang around, of course, show concern. That's what took so long.'

James could hardly believe the good news. Then he remembered how ill the girl had seemed.

'Is she all right? Surely they examined her? No way they didn't.'

Ted looked straight at him. James feared he might have bad news about the girl.

'What is it, Ted? She isn't dead, is she?'

Ted raked a hand through his hair, rubbed his jaw.

'Nowhere near it.' He stared out at the night sky as though he was searching the stars for an answer to a mystery. 'Once she was in a side room she made a miraculous recovery. The doctor who examined her couldn't find a thing wrong but insisted she was taken to hospital for observation. All that worry and that's how it ended.'

'I was sure the pellets had burst inside her. That's the way it looked.'

Ted shrugged. 'They scanned her for drugs, man. Nothing showed.'

James's mouth dropped open. This was too good to be true. 'Maybe in hospital,' James mused. 'Maybe they'll find them when they examine her there.'

'Could be, but ...'

'But what?'

Ted screwed his eyes up tight. Something was obviously confusing him. After a few seconds, he opened them wide and spoke.

'The girl's behaviour is what. She seemed happier, as though the worst was over as soon as they got her in to that side room. She should have been out of her mind but she was … smiling.'

James was equally puzzled, didn't know what to say. If the girl wasn't carrying what had it all been about?

Ted said, 'If the hospital find drugs in her—'

James anticipated him. 'I don't think she'll talk anyway. If she did, those men weren't above killing her family, or anyone connected to her. She'll know that.'

'But the police might persuade her and then we've had it.'

'I think the odds are well in our favour. If we haven't heard anything in the next few days, I think we can consider ourselves home and dry.'

'Home and dry,' Ted repeated, his voice forlorn. 'I like the sound of that.'

James turned the ignition key, started the engine. 'Let's head home anyway, and pray it goes the way we want it to.'

'Amen to that!' Ted said as the car pulled away.

19

THEY TOOK TURNS driving, one trying to sleep while the other drove through the darkness back to Middlesbrough. When dawn swept the landscape the sights became familiar. They both felt better; they'd made it home and there was comfort in that. Five days ago when they'd started out, though it hadn't been voiced neither was sure he'd see the town again, at least not as a free man.

The flat looked just the same. But James felt something about it had changed; the vibes it gave him were different. He wondered if Ted had that same feeling, or whether it was just him. It was something to do with his recent experiences. Previously he had regarded it as a happy haven, associated with his first real independence. Now the memories had been spoiled. What had happened was going to change for ever the way they looked back at their time as students. With a profound feeling of melancholy he realized that he would be glad to move on. The prospect of marrying, the settled life which would go with marriage to Liz, held great appeal.

Ted made a pot of tea and, since they had no food in, they made do with a packet of digestive biscuits. After the long journey the tea revived them, but they were both bone weary.

Ted yawned. 'We need to catch up on our kip, mate. Soon as I've drunk this tea, I'm for bed. Think I'll be able to sleep for England now we're home.'

'The sleep of the just,' James said.

The words were hardly spoken when they heard someone banging on the front door. Ted froze, his mug halfway to his mouth. They stared at each other, not knowing what to do. James felt as though all the blood in his body was rushing to his head.

Ted dropped his digestive on to the table, spat out a volley of crumbs as he spoke.

'Nobody bangs that loud. It has to be the police. They're on to us, James.'

The same thought ricocheted around James's head. He forced a calmness he didn't feel and rose wearily from the chair.

'I'll go and see.'

As though his body was encased in a straitjacket, Ted sat bolt upright and watched him leave the kitchen.

The banging was growing louder as James made his way down the hall. If it wasn't the police, whoever it was must be on urgent business. Taking a deep breath, he steeled himself and unbolted the door.

A black man was standing on the doorstep, dreadlocks cascading from his white woollen hat like snakes from a pile of snow. He raised his eyebrows at James and smiled sardonically. Cocking his head insolently, he jerked a thumb over his shoulder. James noticed a Mercedes parked on the far side of the road. He could see four men inside but couldn't make out their faces.

'The man's here. He come for the suitcases.'

James stared at him. What was this? He knew too well whom he meant by the 'man', but what was this about suitcases? Before he had time to respond, a figure in a grey hood emerged from the car, sprinted across the road and up the path.

The man's momentum took him through the doorway, brushing James aside. Dreadlocks followed him in. Bemused,

James shrank back against the wall and they turned on him, crowding the passage with their physical bulk. The hood came off and James found himself staring into the wild, compelling eyes of the 'man'. Ted chose that moment to enter the hall and Dreadlocks spun to face him.

'You got guests,' he rapped. 'Stay where you are.'

'What happen to the girl?' the man snapped at James, a sharp prod in the chest giving emphasis to each word. His face was so close James could see red veins in the whites of his eyes like rivers of blood in an Arctic landscape.

It took a moment for James to gather his wits. With a quiver in his voice, he said, 'She was ill in customs. They took her away to hospital – but we think she was OK.'

The man slapped James hard with the flat of his hand. His cheek burned with pain and humiliation. Ted shouted in protest. Dreadlocks warned him to shut it or he'd get worse.

'Not her, fool. The other one. What you done with her?'

Perplexed, James realized then that he meant the girl who had accompanied him. A chill ran through his body, its icy fingers penetrating to his core. The girl must have disappeared and they must suspect he was involved. Why else would they come?

'I left her at the airport. That was the last I saw of her. Why would we want her? We just want to be out of it. We kept our part of the bargain, so just let us be.'

The man stepped back, looked James up and down, weighing what he had been told. The anger in his eyes died a little, went from a blazing fire to smoking embers, but James could tell it could flare again as easily as a struck match.

'She didn't turn up where she was supposed. You know anything 'bout that? You know where she might be?'

Relieved that the man had eased back on the pressure, James shook his head.

'No! But the other girl was in a bad way and the customs took her to hospital.' He paused, 'If the sick girl talks—'

A thoughtful look appeared in the man's face. He raised a finger, waved it back and forth in front of James's face like a pendulum.

'No worries.'

James couldn't comprehend his lack of concern. Then a thought struck him.

'She's not dead?' he gasped.

'I said no worries. The girl did good, took the attention away. She wasn't carrying, man. It was the other one.'

Like a boxer winded by a low blow, James slumped against the wall. So Ted's girl had just been a decoy. Judging from her distress at the time, he doubted that the girl who had accompanied him knew that part of the plan. It had worked because she'd got safely through. Afterwards she must have panicked, decided she'd had enough and run off on her own.

'You didn't tell her what was going to happen, did you? It scared her and she ran. You didn't allow for that.'

The man ignored his comment and barked. 'Go get your suitcases.'

James frowned. Puzzled by the command, he stared at the man. A moment ago it had all been about the girl. What was this about suitcases?

'Why do you want them?' he stuttered.

'Jus' do it!'

Knowing it was useless to argue, he made his way to the bedroom, Dreadlock on his heels. He picked up both suitcases carried them back into the hall. The man nodded at Dreadlocks who opened them up and threw the contents on to the floor Producing a knife from his pocket, he kneeled down and cut the lining of Ted's case.

The students exchanged worried glances. It wasn't difficult

for either of them to imagine what Dreadlocks was seeking but it seemed too bizarre to be true.

Ted's suitcase yielded nothing and was discarded. Then Dreadlocks started on James's case. When he'd finished slicing he gave a satisfied smile. James looked over his shoulder and saw what had pleased him. Sitting snugly beneath the lining was a line of small bags held down by tape.

A tremor ran up and down James's spine. All that talk of no risk! He'd been taken for a fool, a fool who'd have merited a long prison sentence if his case had been searched, for there could be no doubt those bags contained drugs. In spite of the man's intimidating closeness to him, he couldn't contain his outrage.

'You lied, you bastard. All that about no danger and all the time ...' Words failed him as he pointed at the drugs. 'This!'

The man laughed in his face. 'Welcome to the real world, boy. Where you bin all these years? You go round believin' everything you told?' He pointed to Ted. 'Him and his woman create the diversion to help you and your woman through. Be grateful – it work.'

James sat on his anger. What was done was done. Anything he said was pointless now. Besides, the man had power over them. Put him in a bad enough mood and he could turn nasty; either that or find a way to let the police know they were his cousin's murderers.

'Well, it's finished now,' he said, his voice shaking. 'We know nothing about the girl, so take what you came for and let us be.'

The man lowered his head, stared at him from under his eyebrows, like a wild animal weighing up its prey.

'Best you be telling me the truth. You don't know where she be? That right. You sure?'

Ted, who'd kept quiet so far, chipped in. 'He told you we don't know.'

The man's eyes moved from one to the other, then he nodded to Dreadlocks, who shut the suitcase and picked it up. The man reached inside his jacket and handed James a card.

'Ring that number if she turn up here like a lost soul.'

Exasperated, James said, 'She doesn't know where I live, so that's an impossibility.'

The gangster made his way to the door, stopped to allow Dreadlocks to pass by, then turned to face them once again.

'I got my cousin's body on ice. If I hear you talk to police, the dead man rise to haunt you. Or maybe I beat him to it.'

'We were the ones who kept our side of the bargain,' James said.

Ted added, 'We're finished with you. We don't ever want to see you again.'

The man's lip curled. 'Let's hope you got nothing going with that girl. For your sake, best she done her own thing.'

With that parting shot he pulled his hood up and stepped outside. James and Ted watched the two gangsters cross the road. Once they were inside the Mercedes it shot off down the street. James followed Ted back into the kitchen. Stunned by the latest turn of events, they sat in silence. James's sense of relief at having survived was short-lived. As if he needed reminding, the gangster had just re-emphasized that he was a murderer. That was something he would have to carry with him to the end of his days. He glanced at Ted who looked badly shaken.

James said, 'We have to drive the whole business out of our minds or it'll send us mad.'

Ted's eyes were melancholy. 'It won't be easy to do that.'

'It's what we have to do.'

Ted shook his head in a way that suggested he'd lost something precious, doubted he'd ever find it again. He wandered over to the sink, turned on the tap and splashed water over his face. When he turned around small droplets were running down his cheeks like tears. James wasn't sure there weren't some tears there.

'Nothing else that happens to us in life can be as bad,' Ted said, trailing a sleeve across his face. 'From now on, it has to be better for us.'

'Of course it has,' James agreed, but he could hear a false note in his voice.

20

THE FOLLOWING AFTERNOON James and Ted decided to go and see Hickson. They found Elizabeth seated beside his bed. That was no surprise because they had met her in the students' union in the morning for a coffee and she'd told them she'd be visiting. What did surprise James was the body language on show. Liz's fists were clenched. Hickson was pointing a finger and his face was red and angry. James sensed tension in the air. He tried to hear what they were saying, but before he could gather the gist they spotted him and moved apart. He noticed Liz's body was rigid, her smile forced. He didn't have a chance to comment because she sprang instantly to her feet, gave him a peck on the cheek, then greeted Ted who was a step behind him.

'Would you believe it,' she said, fingers fidgeting. 'He's arguing politics with me like he always does. Badly of course, but I suppose it's a sign he's feeling much better.'

The hard glint left Hickson's eyes. Like a fading sunset, the angry red in his face retreated into the roots of his red hair.

'We're miles apart, as usual,' he said, staring hard at Liz. 'But she'll come round.'

Liz snorted. 'This lady's not for turning. Some things are set in stone.' She took Ted's arm. 'Anyway, one visitor at a time's enough and I'm afraid I've exhausted you. Take me for a coffee Ted; let James and Dave have a chinwag?'

When the cousins had left the room, James pulled up a chair. He wondered whether this was the time to tell Hickson what really happened that night in the yard. But what good would it do, really? The nurse had told him he'd had no more recall. Letting sleeping dogs lie might be better. Besides, after the recent travails, he wasn't as sure of his flatmate as he'd been in the past. There might be an angry reaction or worse.

Hickson's voice cut into his thoughts. 'Nice tan, old son. What's with you swanning off to Trinidad while your mate is laid up on his sickbed? I'm dead jealous, by the way.'

'Spur of the moment thing,' James came back at him. 'They assured us you were going to be all right and we were both depressed by what had happened. We just needed to get away.'

'Money no object for the rich boys, eh? What was wrong with Blackpool?'

James smiled weakly. 'Liz was right. You must be feeling better. Can't be long before they let you loose on the world again.'

Hickson sighed 'Another two weeks, I'm afraid. Imagine how my pride is hurting, living it up on the NHS like this.'

'I'm told you haven't remembered anything more about that night?'

''Fraid not. The doctors aren't sure I'll ever remember. Apparently that happens in some cases.'

James leaned towards him. 'Maybe it's better if you don't remember. Be like a nightmare revisited, wouldn't it?'

Hickson nodded, was silent for moment, then cocked his head to one side and looked straight into James's eyes. 'You know I lost my mobile that night. I suppose it's trivial, everything considered, but it was my link with the world.'

'Probably stolen,' James answered, surprising himself how easily the lie slipped off his tongue. 'Whoever attacked you took away your ecstasy tablets as well. Must have been out of it because he scattered them in the alley. The police told you, didn't they?'

Hickson grimaced. 'It all looked suspicious, I suppose, but not damning.' He shot James a knowing look. 'Luckily, unlike my friends, I didn't pop any pills that night, so when the docs tested me I was OK.'

James, not enjoying the reminder that he had indulged, reddened. If they had been on the scene when Hickson was picked up, the police could easily have tested them and their careers might have been finished before they started.

A silence developed between them. James looked away, let his eyes roam. He was thinking that, though he'd been through hell, his luck had held to some extent. He had to hope that yesterday's episode was the last of the business. He brought his gaze back to Hickson, and just for a moment thought he saw something move behind his eyes, like a sly creature that lives under water and never surfaces. It skittered away quickly but there was something disturbing about it. He started to wonder if he had imagined it.

Out of the blue, Hickson commented, 'I'll never be as lucky as you and Ted, you know.'

James frowned, disconcerted by his tone of voice, which seemed to encompass a mix of jealousy and melancholia. He hoped he was wrong about the jealousy. Melancholia he could forgive him for. Hickson had been lying in this hospital bed for too long, must be bored stiff. Was the jealousy he thought he detected caused by Hickson's belief that his flatmates had just returned from an enjoyable, exotic holiday?

The conversation became stilted. Hickson seemed to be tiring quickly. His eyelids started to droop, James noticed. He decided he'd better leave. Patting Hickson's shoulder, he started to rise.

'You're ready for a rest,' he said. 'Would you like me to send Ted in for a moment before we go?'

Hickson yawned. 'No offence, but I'm feeling tired. Tell Ted we'll have a chat next time, will you?'

James walked out feeling vaguely disturbed. Though he couldn't define it, something about his friend was different. A void seemed to have opened between them, one he'd found it difficult to traverse. Was it the bang on the head that had changed him, or was the change in himself rather than Hickson? Had recent events altered his own personality, introduced an element of paranoia? He supposed the suspicion that Hickson was more involved with dodgy characters than he'd led them to believe was at the back of his mind, nagging away. When he was better they could tackle him about that, clear the air once and for all.

He found Liz and Ted in the coffee bar, heads together in earnest conversation. They fell silent the second they saw him and, from their secretive glances at each other, he felt sure he could well be the subject under discussion. Or was that the paranoia kicking in again? Feeling slightly embarrassed, he told Ted that Hickson was too exhausted to see him, was best left to rest.

They walked to the main doors with Liz. Once they were outside Ted said he'd go ahead and fetch the car, leaving James to escort Liz to her vehicle which was parked much closer. When he was alone with Liz, James remembered the awkwardness earlier between Hickson and her. His curiosity got the better of him and he decided to ask her outright.

'You and Hickson had a big argument tonight,' he ventured. 'I could smell it in the air. I don't think it was about politics either, because that subject has been exhausted between you two long ago. Politics was just a cover-up, wasn't it?'

'The learned counsel has seen right through me,' she said in a sarcastic tone, raising her eyebrows. 'How perspicacious he is.'

A little put out, James mumbled, 'You don't have to tell me if you don't want to.'

'Don't worry, I'm not going to!' she snapped. Then, suddenly, her expression softened and a twinkle came into her eye. 'Especially when I've more important things to tell you.'

It dawned on him what she was referring to and he blurted out, 'You've decided, haven't you?'

She smiled and took his hand. Her touch felt so light and comforting it seemed to melt away all his troubles. If her decision was the one he was hoping for, she might be able to lead him back to the place where he'd been before his troubles started, might help him find himself again.

'I've thought hard,' she said, gazing into his eyes, 'and my answer is definitely in the affirmative. I want a short engagement, then marriage, James.'

He let out a sigh and wrapped his arms around her. 'Thank God for that. I don't know what I'd have done if you'd said no.'

When they broke away, she looked up at him with a quizzical expression.

'What I want to know is what happened in Trinidad that prompted you to ask? Was it a mystical happening, a voodoo witch doctor casting a spell?' She giggled. 'Or just too much rum?'

Affecting a glum expression, he answered, 'You do me a great disservice, madam, with a travesty of the facts.'

She laughed. 'Come on James, seriously?'

'Well, it wasn't the place. It was me. I suddenly knew I wanted to be more settled, have an anchor in my life and you are the one I love. You know that.'

She touched his cheek. 'James, that's nice. But you do know that, apart from all the romantic stuff, I expect to be kept in the manner to which I am accustomed. I expect you to be a big success, you know.'

Not quite sure how serious she was, James gave a hesitant laugh. 'So all I'm to be is a meal ticket?'

She tossed her hair back over her shoulder, tilted her head to look at him.

'My family is pretty well off, as is yours. We can already afford meals, James, can't we? It's a ticket to life's big banquets I'm after. You and I will be at the high table, my love.'

James laughed, not taking her too seriously. Ambition was a good thing in your wife, he supposed. Before he could comment, Ted drove up and wound the driver's window down.

James grinned 'Well, old girl, here's the chauffeur. Going to tell him?'

Ted grinned. 'Already has. Suppose we're sort of related now. I was against corrupting our bloodline, of course, but she wouldn't listen.'

In a light-hearted mood, they chatted idly for a few minutes. At last Liz decided she had to go and climbed into her car. She waved as she pulled away. James, his spirits improved, got in beside his friend.

'You think I've done the right thing, don't you, Ted?'

Ted frowned as he changed gear. 'She's my cousin. What do you expect me to say? You shouldn't have asked her if you're not sure.' After a brief silence, he added. 'Curb that ambition of hers a bit and she'll be fine for you, as you will be for her. I'm sure of it.'

James nodded. 'I know she's ambitious. Youth is ambition, I suppose.' He decided to change the subject. 'There was something going on between her and Dave when we walked in. She said they were arguing politics but I don't think so. Did she say?'

'Not a word to me.' Ted paused. 'I take it you didn't tell Dave what really happened that night?'

James shook his head. 'He still can't remember much and I decided to let sleeping dogs lie; for now, anyway.' He glanced across at Ted. 'Maybe it would be better if we don't tell him?'

Ted's lips pulled back in a grimace. 'Maybe you're right. Maybe his ignorance is our bliss.'

21

D. I. DAVIS PARKED next to the kerb, turned off the engine and rubbed his tired eyes. Frustrated as well as fatigued, he felt like the Dutch boy with his finger in the dyke, holding back threatening waters. He told himself that all policemen experienced this at times. Whatever they did individually or collectively, they were only scratching at the surface. Non-co-operation was a fact of life in his trade. Right now the streets weren't even whispering. None of his snouts were giving him anything and the street girls of his acquaintance were unusually subdued. That grisly, severed head was shouting the odds louder than its former owner ever had in life, and that was saying something. A stranglehold lay on the town, one he'd break in the end. It was the damage meantime, his responsibility to prevent it, that concerned him.

He lifted his briefcase off the passenger seat, removed the file containing the photograph and record sheet. For a moment he hesitated, glancing out of the window at the window of the students' flat. Should he bother with this now or come back some other time? Darkness was creeping in and this matter was low priority in his list of things to do. He didn't figure the two students would recognize Winston anyway. On his last visit, they hadn't acknowledged knowing the West Indian. Yet, he supposed, there was just a faint chance the photograph taken near the pub from the CCTV tape would spark a memory.

Winston Smart was West Indian in origin, therefore possibly, just possibly, linked to Yardies, and ecstasy tablets had been found in the alley suggesting connections to the drug trade. It wasn't much really and it was by no means certain that Winston was the attacker.

What finally drove him out of the car and up the path for his last effort of the day was the knowledge of what Yardies, supplying crack cocaine on a large scale, could do to the town. He knew that when the drug had first hit New York, forty per cent of murders had been crack-related. To stifle it here, before its poisonous tentacles gripped, was vital; he'd be failing in his duty if he didn't follow up any clue, no matter how inconsequential it might seem, no matter how dispirited he felt.

The taller, well-built student answered the door at the third ring. In the moment of recognition, Davis thought he saw something in the student's face that made him feel as welcome as a meat-eater at a vegetarians' convention. It disappeared in an instant, consumed by a weak smile.

'James, isn't it?' Davis chirped with a brightness he didn't feel.

'Inspector,' James said. His smile broadened but never reached his eyes. 'This is a surprise. Are you here because you've found the person who beat up our friend?'

Davis returned the smile, knowing it was as much an impostor as the one he'd received. 'Appreciate it if I could come in for a minute,' he said. 'Like you and your mate to look at a photograph.'

Frowning, James stood back. 'Of course. We're in the kitchen.'

The smell of fried bacon teased Davis's nostrils and tastebuds as he followed James down the hall. The second student, Ted by name as he recalled, was sitting at the kitchen table. The mother of all fry-ups sat on a plate in front of him. The sight and smell teased his own stomach and he heard it cry out for satisfaction. All he had eaten since breakfast was a cheese roll and he vowed to have a fry-up himself when he got home. Hang the calories for once.

When Ted saw the visitor he paused, fork halfway to his mouth, a giant mushroom impaled on the prongs. His face reddened until it wasn't far from the shade of the tomatoes piled on his plate. He looked agitated. Davis wondered what it was he had to be embarrassed about? He doubted it was being caught in his gluttony. True, policemen sometimes had a certain effect just by being policemen, as though their presence alone had the power to induce a primitive instinct, something to do with guilt complexes, even in the innocent. But this young man was going to be a lawyer soon. In Davis's experience they weren't shy of policemen. Was this young man the exception who proved the rule?

James piped up. 'The inspector's got a photo he wants us to look at.'

Ted seemed to relax. He put the mushroom in his mouth and twirled his fork in the air. 'Then you must have found the one you think attacked Dave?'

Davis shook his head. 'Not yet.' He felt inside the file, brought out a photograph of Winston and laid it on the table. 'This fellow was caught on CCTV pretty close to the scene. As you can see, he's had a bit of damage done to him. Did you see him that night or perhaps on another occasion?'

The two students studied the photograph, then looked at each other and shook their heads.

'Afraid we haven't seen him before,' James announced. 'Have you shown it to our pal?'

'No, not yet, but I will. It was just that I was passing on my way home and thought I'd give it a go with you fellers.'

'Sorry to disappoint you,' Ted said. 'I hope you soon catch the animal who did it.'

The kitchen suddenly grew darker and James switched the light on. In the brighter light, Davis realized what it was that was different about the two lads since his last visit. It had been nagging at the back of his mind. Now he knew. Both were sporting suntans; genuine or fake he couldn't be sure. It seemed strange because the weather recently had been awful, the sun making only fleeting visits and the cold north–east wind likely to deliver wind chill.

Keeping his tone light-hearted, he gave his curiosity rein. 'You lads look uncommonly healthy. Glowing, in fact. Don't tell me they've opened one of those suntan studios in this area.'

He watched them exchange glances, a habit of theirs which was beginning to grate with him. It had been a simple, straightforward comment but you'd think a million pounds was riding on the reply. He felt like a quizmaster dangling a cheque before their eyes, neither man being prepared to commit to an answer without the other's assent in case it was the wrong one and they would have cause for regret later. In his experience, youth was never so overly serious without good cause.

'We've been away for a few days,' Ted muttered eventually, a surliness in his tone, as though Davis had no right to be so nosy.

The policeman raised a quizzical eyebrow. He was puzzled on two counts. First, there wasn't a place in the country where they could have gained a tan like that over the past week, not even on the south coast which had been blighted by unusually grey skies. On the second count, their flatmate was in hospital in a right state, so what were they doing going off? Maybe he'd got it wrong. Flatmates didn't have to be big buddies. Yet they'd given him that impression, and the landlord of the Blacksmith had told him the three were always together.

'Lucky blighters,' he commented, then added, 'Student exchange or something, was it?'

The silence weighed heavily as he watched the look pass between them again. Perhaps they had no individual initiative, could only function in unison, like twins he had heard about. Pretending amusement, he baited them.

'Secret rendezvous, was it? From the look on your faces, it must have been some mission. If I tell you, I have to kill you, sort of thing?'

'Trinidad, actually,' James answered, using the same self-defensive tone that his friend had used a moment earlier. 'A short break to recover from the strain of our final exams. Our parents treated us.'

His curiosity aroused, Davis whistled. 'All that way for a short break. Some of us should be so lucky, eh?'

'Bit silly of us really, I suppose.' Ted came back at him in a quiet, muffled voice. He kept his eyes down, staring at his plate. 'One of those mad things students do. But then, we are students. It's part of the job description.'

'But you enjoyed it. That's what counts,' Davis said, feigning empathy. He kept on the subject. 'Fly from Newcastle, did you?'

Slight hesitation, then James answered, 'Bristol, actually. The flight times were convenient. Newcastle don't do direct flights.'

As James was speaking, Davis tried to make connections. Winston Smart was from Jamaica originally, but Trinidad was close and drug-smuggling was rife in most of the Caribbean islands. Was it just possible these two intelligent young men, and their friend in hospital, could be connected through Winston to the drug trade? Had there been an argument with him over drugs that night in the yard, an argument that had ended in violence?

He hauled back his thoughts. Was he that desperate? He was

surely stretching it, clutching at straws, making a fiction in his mind from scraps. They were so young, these two. Yet he couldn't dismiss the idea entirely. Sometimes even the smallest coincidence was trying to tell you something and you'd better not ignore it or it would mock you later for your complacency.

With a casual air he picked the photograph up from the table and returned it to the folder.

'Sorry to interrupt your tea, lads.'

Ted glanced up at him. Davis thought he looked relieved. 'That's OK. Anything that might help find the fellow who beat Dave up needs investigating. We understand that. Sorry it's been a wasted trip.'

'Oh, I don't know about wasted.' Davis grinned and watched their faces closely. 'I have found some food for thought, you know.'

He could have sworn he'd just announced a death. He'd seen haunted eyes like theirs before, mainly when criminals realized they were facing years in prison; these lads' eyes had the same look now.

Ted stuttered. 'I – I don't understand.'

James kept quiet but from the set of his mouth Davis could tell his teeth were biting against the inside of his lower lip, a sign of his apprehension. With slow deliberation he let his eyes drift from one to the other, then back again, keeping the line he'd cast taut to see what reaction he'd get. When it was so taut he could hold it no longer, he pointed to Ted's plate.

'You've reconverted me, son. Forgotten what it's like to have a good old fry-up. Been years, in fact. When I get home, I'm going to have the mother of all fry-ups and hang the calorie count the wife's been pushing.'

He could see the strain sliding off them as evidently as the grease running off the bacon on Ted's plate. It was just another little sign to fuel his policeman's instinct that something wasn't quite right here. Of course, it could be something unrelated to the case altogether, but something was off key. He was convinced of it. Under the calm, jovial exterior that they were doing their best to project, these two lads were far too wound up.

James followed him to the door and they said a polite farewell on the doorstep. He got in the car and sat for a moment reflecting on what he had seen and heard in the flat. None of his thoughts was anywhere near conclusive but they were enough to merit further exploration into what was going on in the lives of the two students.

Back inside the flat, James didn't want to show his pal how worried he was. He needed to occupy himself in order to divert his mind, help release the tension, so he went straight to the sink and started on the washing-up. Ted said nothing, just watched, but James sensed his silent brooding.

His hands deep in water, James said, 'Why the hell did we tell him we'd been to Trinidad?'

Ted pushed his plate away, leaned an elbow on the table and mumbled, 'He asked us, didn't he?'

James made a clatter with the dishes and snapped, 'We could have told him anything.'

Ted sighed. 'You mean we could have lied to him. Come on, mate! That would have been too risky.'

James wiped sweat from his brow. 'Do you think he was suspicious? It does seem strange taking a trip to Trinidad for only five days, especially so with pal Hickson in hospital.'

'He believed that spur of the moment stuff, didn't he?'

James shrugged. 'Can't be sure.' He started to dry one of the plates. 'Anyway, are we in denial here? He had a picture of the man we killed and we haven't mentioned that. I nearly died when I saw that face.'

'So did I,' Ted said, his voice muted. 'But that's all he has – a picture. If those gangsters keep their bargain there'll be no body. It's been a week now and so far—'

Before he could say more James interrupted him. 'He was showing us a picture of a West Indian, wasn't he?'

'So what?'

'We've just returned from the Caribbean, haven't we?'

Ted's voice rose. 'You're being really paranoid now. We can't afford to be like that. You said it yourself. We've got to hold it together or we'll go under.'

James held up his hands. 'OK! Sorry mate. You're right.'

Usually it was he, not Ted, who took the lead, kept his cool. This was role reversal. He knew it was because something in the policeman's manner had bothered him, something that perhaps Ted hadn't perceived. He hoped his intuition was wrong, that his suspicion that there were devious undercurrents in the policeman's questions was, as Ted had just suggested, his own paranoia kicking in.

22

THE POLICE STATION sat in the heart of Middlesbrough, only yards off the central square, which was bordered by the old library and town hall. The magistrates' court was situated in the town hall building. Davis parked nearby, got out of the car and watched the early-morning sun stretching its golden fingers across the square. Like fat old actors seeking the spotlight, a crowd of pigeons, habitual residents of the square, waddled out of the shadows into the sun and preened themselves. One came close to his feet so that he could hear a contented gurgling. They appeared not to have a care in the world, those pigeons, and he envied them their lazy contentment.

As he started to walk towards the police station a movement on the town hall roof caught his eye. Glancing up, he noticed a large bird perched there like a regal figure looking down on its kingdom. He remembered he'd read something in the *Evening Gazette* about an escaped bird of prey that had taken up residence on the roof. In the same moment as the thought came to him the bird spread its wings and swooped, like a dive-bomber coming out of the sun. The fat pigeon it targeted had no chance. Sharp talons dug into its plump body, lifted it off the ground and carried it away.

Davis shook his head sadly. It was ironic that even above the courts of justice there was a predator waiting for its chance. The students he'd visited last night came to mind. In many ways they seemed so young and innocent. But were they really? Could they be innocents caught up in something? He was determined to find out by following a scent he thought he'd caught last night.

DC Harland was at her desk when he walked in. She looked up, surprised to see anyone else in so early.

'Out for promotion, are we?' he teased. 'Just wait until you're married with kids to turn out.'

'You're married,' she shot back at him. 'What happened? Have a row with your wife and decide to come in early to escape the fall-out.'

Davis grinned. 'Actually, I followed a minor lead yesterday. It threw up possibilities which I wanted to follow up quickly. There's something bugging me, an itch I want to scratch.' He yawned. 'It kept me awake.'

She leaned back. 'Come on then, I'm all ears.'

He told her about the students, their nervousness and their impulse trip to Trinidad when their pal was in hospital, his hunch that they could be connected in some way to the Jamaican whose picture he'd shown them. This morning, laid out coldly, it sounded more implausible than it had the night before, but he figured that that was because you had to have been there with them in the kitchen to appreciate his suspicions.

'So, you see, I'm glad you're in early, all bright-eyed and bushy-tailed, because I want you to get on to Bristol airport, check out that they did fly from there. Ask if they can send CCTV footage of the lads going through customs, outward and inward flights.'

Harland groaned. 'So it's me who's to scratch that itch for you. Hope these young men are worth the trouble.'

'Privilege of rank, having your itches scratched,' Davis said.

'And while you're at it arrange a fax to the Royal Jamaican Police – and contact Interpol.' He opened his briefcase, took out the file on Winston Smart and laid it in front of her. 'The guy in the photographs has connections in Jamaica, but it's particularly Bradley, the bad boy cousin who's mentioned in the file who interests me. Get what you can, Diane, please.'

Harland supped at her coffee, holding her mug with one hand, opening the file with the other. 'You do realize it could take time, don't you?' She sighed and mumbled, 'At least you said please.'

'It could take the Boro' years to win the premiership – if ever,' he answered. 'But they keep trying. There's your inspiration.'

She glanced at him from under her eyebrows. 'Not much inspiration there, but for premiership wages I'd sprout wings and fly to the Caribbean for you.'

He left her to get on with it and made his way from the open-plan offices to his own more private office, which he preferred because there were no distractions. He took his jacket off, put his feet up on the desk and waded through the latest batch of paperwork. Two pieces, amongst a host of instantly forgettable trivia, caught his interest. On the day of Fat Stan's murder, a witness had seen three black men getting out of a car two streets away from his flat. Better still, another witness had reported seeing three men of the same description approaching the flats. Though that witness couldn't give an exact time, she estimated it was within an hour of Stan taking the long drop.

Davis rubbed his chin thoughtfully as he considered this latest information. London had always been the Yardies' main field of operation in this country but they had become more nomadic in recent years. In fact, Bristol, whose airport the students had flown from, was probably their latest stronghold. They'd infected places in Scotland in a big way too. He shook his head. It seemed almost beyond the bounds of possibility that the fresh faced students could be tied up with scum like that.

23

JAMES PLUCKED THE sponge from the bucket of soapy water, shoved it to and fro on the car bonnet. He was trying to forget Davis's visit but it continued to replay in his head. Even when he managed to eliminate the policeman from his thoughts, like a substitute who can't wait to come on to the field to bolster the attack, the knowledge that he was a murderer swept into his brain. He wondered whether he would ever master that guilty feeling, function like a normal human being again. In the end though, what choice did he have? That fateful night in the yard they'd embarked on a road of no return.

The car was parked on the driveway. He was facing the house, the pavement and road here behind him. Suddenly he had a peculiar sense that someone was watching him from the pavement. A tingling sensation ran up and down his spine. Had Ted returned early from his trip to see a friend? He turned sharply, couldn't see anybody and gave himself a mental ticking-off. Was paranoia an infection that spread into everything you did, every facet of your life? Did it have physical manifestations, conjure ghosts? He turned back to the car; as he did so he caught a movement at the edge of his vision and spun round again.

The wide-brimmed, flowery hat was pulled low, burying the face in shadow, so that it was difficult to put an age to the female who was standing there half-hidden by the hedge. He had the impression she was staring at him. Before she moved away and the hedge hid her completely he had time to notice that her clothes were baggy, but little else. He figured she must be just be a passer-by, perhaps a dog-walker who'd paused for a moment.

He dismissed the incident, wrung out the sponge and attacked the car with renewed vigour. When he'd worked his way right round, he straightened up and pushed his palms into the small of his back to ease aching muscles. That was when he saw her again. He froze on the spot, his body arched like a bow. This time she did not move away, simply stood there staring, like a little child unsure of herself at the school gates on her first day.

When, eventually, her hands reached up and removed the hat he recognized her instantly. The shock made him drop the sponge. Her presence there seemed so out of time and place that for a moment he thought his mind was playing a cruel trick. The blood in his head pounded. He stepped backwards, slipped in a pool of soapy water and almost went over.

She put the hat back on and came towards him carrying her hold-all over her shoulder. Soapy suds swirled round her feet, soaking her open sandals. James saw she was wearing no make-up and her face was more haggard than before. Her eyes, full of doubt, never left his for a moment, as though she wasn't sure what reaction to expect from him but, regardless, was determined to do what she'd come here to do.

James's initial surprise gave way to anger. When the girl had walked away from him at the airport he hadn't expected to ever see her again. Not in this lifetime. But here she was, a walking time-bomb advancing up the driveway. What the hell was she playing at?

She stopped in front of him, looked up into his face, bottom lip quivering, a schoolgirl again in the presence of an irate headmaster. 'Saw your address on your suitcase, had nowhere to go for help. I thought—'

James held up his hand to stop her. He was past himself. His address on his case! A little thing like that. A little thing that could be so deadly. It had led this foolish girl right to his door. If those gangsters found her here, they'd think the meeting was arranged, that he was helping her steal their precious drugs. Fearful that she was being followed, he looked beyond her to the street, his senses coming alive. Maybe they were watching right now. Maybe they'd expected this to happen. First priority, he had to get her out of sight. Second priority, he had to get rid of her, get her out of his life. Those thoughts driving him, he grabbed her arm, dragged her up the path like a naughty child, pushed her inside the door.

In the sanctuary of the hallway she placed the hold-all on the floor, took off that ludicrous hat and turned to face him, a pleading look in her eyes. He slammed the door with all his force and she shrank away from him when she saw how angry he was.

'Damn you,' he said. 'Why did you have to come to me? Don't you know what you've done? They've been here, looking for you.' He saw her tears coming, but didn't let up. 'Why did you do it? Why?'

Rubbing her eyes, she bent down, opened the hold-all. She put her hand inside and pulled out a bag of white powder. Like a child offering to share a new toy to make everything all right again, she held it towards him. But there was nothing of childish innocence about that toy. It was more like a poisoned chalice and, only too aware of what it was she was offering, he glared at her.

'You think I'm a dealer? Is that it? You've pulled some kind of double cross on those guys and you think I'll take that rubbish off your hands?'

More tears flowed from her. The heat of his anger gradually died and he softened towards her. But he didn't let it sway him. She didn't deserve anything from him, this girl. She'd brought danger to his door.

'I panic,' she sobbed. 'I see my friend collapse, lose my nerve, just want to run. It was my first time. They promise me good money if I do it.'

James forced himself to keep calm, tried to think. He didn't like the situation but losing his cool wasn't going to help. In spite of himself, he felt a certain sympathy for the girl. He'd read about girls like her, most of them trapped in poverty, inveigled into smuggling drugs by exploitative gangsters who led them to believe nothing could go wrong, that it was easy money. In a way, he supposed, her experience wasn't unlike their own.

'Follow me,' he said, relenting a little. 'You'll have something to eat and then we'll try to think what to do for the best.'

She dried her tears on her sleeve and followed him into the living room. He sat her down and left her alone while he went to the kitchen to prepare some food. When he returned with a pot of tea and some ham sandwiches, she was asleep in the chair but woke with a start when he put the tray down beside her.

'Now,' he said, settling into a chair. 'I'd like to hear your story, particularly why you've come here. What, in your crazy, mixed-up mind, you believe we can do for you?'

She began hesitantly and he had to prompt her, but she gradually lost her inhibition. As she became more fluent, she told it as though it was all happening to her in the here and now, all over again. Her life in Trinidad had been a harrowing one, years of poverty made worse when both her parents had died a year before, leaving her alone in the world. A series of menial jobs followed, paying just enough to keep her. Then, one night, sitting in a bar feeling lonely and sorry for herself, a guy approached her, offered her £1,000 to carry drugs to England. There was nothing to it, easiest money she'd ever earn. Her morale at its lowest point, confused by the drink he'd plied her with, she agreed. Later in the cold, sober light of day, she'd tried to renege. But the man said the arrangements were made. It was too late for second thoughts. Powerful people would be upset and they'd hurt her. Frightened, she'd agreed to go ahead and, though she might have appeared to be cool and together at the airport, the truth was her insides had been churning.

'Your friend?' James said, moved by her tale but trying to stay cool and detached. 'She got the same treatment, did she?'

'Yes. They introduced us. She was nice to me. That's why I was upset.'

James shook his head. 'Why didn't you go to the police?'

She looked at him with wide eyes, as though that was the stupidest question she'd ever heard.

'Man, those fellers would have killed me. Surely, you know it? They ain't afraid of no police and mercy is jus' weakness in their world.'

James dropped his eyes. He did know about their power to terrorize. The day they'd taken Ted and him he'd been to hell and back. Ruthlessness had oozed, like primordial slime, out of every pore of the men who'd seized them. The memory made him shudder even now. Logic, doing the right thing, didn't always work when you were threatened like that. His own certainties about himself and his world had been challenged and found wanting.

His voice more gentle, he said, 'They came here looking for you, thought you and I made a deal cutting them out. I think I convinced them we didn't but I'm supposed to let them know if you turn up.'

Doubt crept in to her face. Was she sheltering from wolves in a lion's lair? Was the lion feeding her up on ham sandwiches only to gorge upon her later with the other beasts?

James saw the look, said quickly, 'They gave me a number to ring – but don't worry. I won't use it. Perhaps …'

Reassured, she said, 'I had a number to ring in Bristol if it all go wrong. But was too scared to use it.'

'I was going to suggest you could use the phone number they gave me. Tell them how you panicked, arrange to give them their drugs back. They'd listen. Why wouldn't they?'

The girl leaned away, stared disbelievingly.

'Thought you were getting it,' she groaned. 'You can't trust those crazy fellers with your life – my life. Ain't you been hearing me? You met them. Don't you know?'

James sighed long and deep. He thought he'd come up with a way out for all of them but the girl was right. The man would know he'd given her the number to use and that would connect her with him. They were unpredictable enough to punish both of them, thinking they'd conspired, then got cold feet. But what could he do? Every second the girl was here meant danger.

His frustration spilled into his words. 'If you can't go to them and you can't go to the police, what did you expect of me? I've been as much of a pawn in their game as you have. What, in the name of God, can I possibly do to help you?'

She dropped her eyes and a silence ensued. It dragged out as James tried to think of solutions that would guarantee safety for all concerned. He could come up with nothing except the one they'd rejected as too dangerous.

Eventually, a tremor in her voice, she broke the silence. 'I am a stranger in this land. I thought you sell the drugs for me, give me money to buy a ticket to take me back home, maybe a bit more to give me a start.'

'Think again, lady,' he snapped. 'I'm not a drug dealer and I don't want more trouble.'

Her shoulders slumped and her eyes filled up. He figured he'd just destroyed her last remnant of hope. She looked away,. spoke in a plaintive whisper that seemed addressed to invisible presences rather than him.

'Where am I to go? What am I to do?'

He mumbled, 'If you went back to Trinidad, they'd find you there and punish you just the same.'

'Somewhere else,' she said, coming back to herself. 'Not Trinidad. Somewhere in the Caribbean where they wouldn't find me. But I need money to help me get fresh start. If you don't help me …' Her voice trailed off.

James could see the girl was reaching the end of her tether, her desperation was plain to see. She looked so drained. She had obviously seen him as her last hope and now that he wasn't able to help she was caving in. How on earth had she survived these last few days alone in a foreign country, he wondered? Worse to contemplate, what had it been like for her with those drugs inside her stomach? He couldn't even imagine how horrific it must have been wandering around with the knowledge that if one pellet burst it would be curtains for her.

He asked her gently, 'After you ran, where did you go? You didn't know anyone in this country, did you?'

Her voice flat, she explained how she'd had enough money for a taxi from the airport into Bristol. The taxi driver dropped her at a hostel and they'd taken her in for a few nights without too many questions. She'd used what little money she had left to buy laxatives to help expel the fifty pellets of cocaine she was carrying in her stomach. It had taken five days, the anxiety of hiding what she was doing exhausting.

'Afterwards,' she continued, as he listened patiently. 'I tell one of the hostel workers I go to Middlesbrough where I have a friend. Her brother has lorries. She arrange for him to take me so far. Then, another lorry bring me here.'

She stared away for a moment. 'Only thing to do.'

In spite of his own concerns, James's heart went out to her. Living in that hostel, waiting for the drugs to pass out of her body, must have been nerve-racking and physically unpleasant, to say the least. And all her fortitude had been in vain. What madness had made her think he could help her? She'd have been better staying in Bristol where there were plenty of drug dealers. He wanted to tell her to leave but was finding it difficult. She seemed so young and innocent, he couldn't bring himself to just wash his hands of her like that. He needed time to think of a way to help her. Perhaps Ted, when he returned, would have an idea what to do.

'Tonight you stay here,' he announced, hoping he wasn't putting his head in a noose of his own making. 'You can use the spare room. It has a key and it would be best to stay in there and keep it locked in case those men return unexpectedly. There's an old mattress in there you can use. My friend and I will put our heads together and maybe come up with a way out of this mess.'

Her face lit up like the sun coming out from behind a dark cloud. 'Thank you,' she said. 'I am so sorry to bring you trouble.'

He fetched fresh linen and showed her to the spare room. When she was settled he left her there and returned to the living room where he sat with a glass of beer mulling over this latest problem. He hadn't got any further towards a solution when Ted returned. His preoccupation must have been evident because as soon as Ted entered the room he asked what was wrong. James explained, watching fear creep into Ted's face when he realized their troubles weren't over, that there was a bomb in the flat in the form of the girl, waiting to blow their lives apart just when they'd seemed to be back on track.

Stunned, Ted sat down, put his head in his hands. James felt for his friend, knew his morale had plummeted to the depths again.

'There's no end to it, is there?' Ted groaned, raking his cheeks with his fingers. 'Whenever we think we've shaken it off, it jumps right up and takes another bite. God must be punishing us for killing that guy.'

Not wanting to surrender to his own self-pity, James said, 'She's here now. Have you any ideas?'

Ted said nothing for a moment, then, recovering some composure, shook his head.

'We either sell the drug for her as she suggested or send her away, back on to the streets to let her fend for herself. Some choice, isn't it?'

'If the police picked her up they could get it out of her that we're involved,' James told him.

'So do we take another risk and sell the drugs?' Ted moaned, gripping the arms of the chair.

James found the idea equally distasteful. What did they know about selling drugs? Immediately he remembered that they knew someone who might have an idea how to go about it.

'There's a chance Dave can help us.'

Ted grimaced. 'Hickson?'

'Why not? Helping him got us into this mess so now he can help us get out of it. He must have contacts even if they're minor players. He can try to set it up.'

Ted thought about it for a moment. 'It might be worth a try. But he was a minnow, wasn't he? Just bought a little now and again for recreational purposes.'

'Like I said, he'll know someone with contacts up the chain.'

'They'd bite our hands off,' Ted opined. 'How much is it worth, do you think?'

'She reckons she was told fifty thousand but we could sell it for much less. Just enough to provide her air fare home and a little more to give her a fresh start. It's all she wants herself.'

Ted stared into the corner of the room. 'We'd have to keep her out of sight until it's done.'

'She'll want to hide. She's been through quite an ordeal. As long as she knows she'll be going home, she'll co-operate. I'm sure of it.'

They lit the gas fire, sat there in the gloom contemplating the weight of what they were about to do. As the night wore on the shadows on the walls lengthened, like dark, preternatural presences gathering to pronounce the judgement of the ages on them. None of the alternatives they discussed seemed viable.

Ted said, eventually. 'If we do this for her, it will help make up for what we've done, won't it – in a small way?'

For his friend's sake James agreed, but he couldn't see it that way. They'd killed a man. How could anything make up for that? Ted was clutching at straws, trying to appease his conscience. Hickson had told them people would do anything when they were cornered. They'd poured scorn on his opinion but he'd been proved correct. They'd descended into the twilight world outside the law to protect themselves. Now they were about to do so again. When was the roller-coaster going to stop and let them off?

'Let's get to bed and sleep on it,' he said, feeling weary of it all.

As they rose to retire, Ted said, 'This started with us trying to help Dave Hickson. Now he can help us end it.'

'We'll need to tell him the truth now,' James stated, stifling a yawn, 'or a close approximation.'

Later, as he lay in bed, his conscience tormented him. He thought he'd known himself, the rules he lived by, lines he would never cross, no matter what. Now his sense of himself was in pieces. Had they both been fooling themselves into thinking they were stand-up blokes, he wondered, when all the time their characters were entrenched in primal mud. They'd had all the privileges but deep down were they no better than the gangsters?

24

HARRY DAVIS KNOCKED on the door of the pathologist's office, entered when Jim Murray called out. Murray, a pipe-smoker who wouldn't give it up in spite of the barbed comments he received as the campaign against smoking gathered force, was a man Davis respected. Unlike those corpses, to whom he devoted his professional attentions, Murray always looked comfortable in his own skin. Even when he had just cause, he didn't show anger. Davis wondered whether that was because he didn't want to waste energy on things that lost importance seen from the perspective of the mortuary slab where he practised his profession.

As Davis crossed the room, for Murray's benefit he made a point of sniffing the air like a bloodhound on a scent.

'How's the addict?' he remarked. 'The one I can't arrest. The one who leaves a trail of evidence everywhere he goes?'

Murray's face broke into a broad smile. 'Adding my wee bit of pollution to the Teesside air isn't too significant in the grand scheme of things, Harry.'

'Haven't you heard?' Davis said, taking a chair. 'There's salmon finding their way up the River Tees these days and seals are returning to the estuary in droves. Won't be long before the anti-pollution brigade hear about your little enclave of reactionary attitudes. You'll be for it.'

Murray laughed, then his face grew serious. 'There are other kinds of pollution; the kind I've called you in about.'

Davis sat forward. 'I'm sure there are. I'm all ears, Jim.'

Murray cleared his throat. 'Last night our uniformed pals had to arrest a man in Easterside. Apparently this fellow was going crazy, wounded four innocent passers-by with a bread-knife. It took four uniforms to subdue him and he went on struggling for ages. They tell me he seemed to possess superhuman strength.'

'He must have been high. I'll probably end up questioning him.'

'I don't think you will,' Murray said, his mouth forming into a twisted grin, 'unless, that is, your intuitive gifts extend to communicating with the dead. You see, this fellow died last night in a police cell. Drowned in his own vomit.'

Davis shot him a querulous look. 'That means trouble for someone, but it leaves me out of the equation, surely?' He hesitated, realizing the pathologist wouldn't call him in for nothing. 'Or does it?'

Murray leaned back in his chair. 'I tested this fellow's blood, urine, the usual gamut of tests and found a higher concentration of crack cocaine than I've ever seen. Thought you'd want to know that, soon as.'

Davis was silent for a moment. He couldn't say he was at all surprised. He knew prostitutes were being supplied with crack, so it was only a matter of time before it fed in from other tributaries, eventually became a river in flood. It could be that this recent user got his drug from a prostitute.

'Appreciate your telling me. I expected it, truth be told.'

'You're on to something, then?'

'Knew it was coming.' Davis sighed, shook his head. 'But I'm not making much progress finding where from.'

'Like trying to push an elephant to see what it's sitting on,' Murray mused.

Davis rose from his chair. 'Got it in one.'

'So a storm is brewing?'

Davis stood up and walked to the door. 'You should have been a detective,' he said, opening the door and looking back at the pathologist. 'Storm's already hit, I'm afraid. Only a matter of time and it'll be the blood of innocents involved.'

He drove back to police headquarters thinking about those innocent souls wounded by the crazy man. The attacker had paid the price with his life but standing behind him was a line of dealers, all equally guilty in Davis's view. He'd heard all the excuses the scum used; they were providing a service; nobody forced anybody to take drugs; if they didn't deal somebody else would. It sickened him how easily they pulled the blinds down on the deaths they caused and afterwards claim it was nothing to do with them. The really big boys were too ruthless even to make excuses. To them conscience was an alien concept, a word not in their dictionary. Davis wondered when he was going to get a real break, one that would lead him to those shadowy figures, those greedy great white sharks who fed on the weakest, then disappeared into the depths with their spoils.

25

WHEN HE WAS back in his office, Davis sat at the desk, chewed his pencil and stared out over the rooftops. People who didn't know Middlesbrough thought it was an old town, but in truth it was relatively new, had grown up when they discovered iron ore in the nearby Eston Hills, which was the start of a great iron-and-steel industry. The town had been christened the Infant Hercules and the people had endured with great strength, their character forged from hardship. Now, the devil crack cocaine was working its way into that infant's bloodstream with no respect for what had gone before, no respect for Davis's forefathers who'd slaved in the steel works. Like the searing flames from the furnaces, the facts about crack burned their way through his brain; eighty per cent of crack users were addicted within two weeks, compared to seven per cent of cocaine users; to get high took about forty seconds compared to cocaine's thirty minutes; resistance to crack developed quickly so more was needed for the same effect; profits for crack were many times higher.

It was a depressing train of thought. Restless, he stood up and wandered to the window. In the square below, two young men sat on a bench feeding the pigeons. There was kindness in men after all. His thoughts turned to the law students. It was difficult to imagine how youngsters with their opportunities in life could possibly involve themselves in the drugs trade. And yet he was experienced enough to know, where people were concerned, you could never be certain. He'd met murderers more like cherubs on the surface, high court judges with characters as soiled as those they pronounced on. Never judge a book by its cover wasn't a bad maxim in his game.

A rap on the door interrupted his reverie. DC Harland swept in holding a sheaf of papers in one hand. He moved away from the window, spoke before she had a chance to.

'I saw Murray today. He tells me a guy went crazy on crack last night – big concentration in his blood. We've got to knock it on the head.'

'We've seen crack before, haven't we, sir?'

He raised his eyebrows. 'If I'm right, those were flea-bites, Diane.'

Harland placed the papers on his desk and stood back. 'This fax came from the Royal Jamaica Police. Makes interesting reading.'

He sat down and studied the papers. When he'd finished he leaned back, inhaled deeply. Apparently Bradley Smart, Winston's cousin, had spent six years in a Jamaican jail for manslaughter. After his release it had only taken him two weeks to become a suspect in a murder case involving drugs. Before they could arrest him, he'd disappeared. That was three years ago and the police's opinion back then was that he'd absconded to the United Kingdom using a false passport. It was interesting stuff, but one part leapt out of the print, penetrating his brain like a laser beam.

'So the victim in the murder case had his head and arms cut off with a machete, Harland, just like Jack Hudson on the riverbank.'

'Yes, sir. Not exactly a common or garden fetish, lopping heads off, is it?'

Davis curbed his mounting sense of excitement. He didn't

want to read too much into what could be that wanton hand of coincidence. But it was something else to bolster his suspicions. Winston Smart had been in the vicinity the night Dave Hickson had been beaten. Bradley Smart liked to mutilate corpses in the same style used on Jack Hudson. The students' jaunt had been to Trinidad, only a kick in the backside away from Jamaica. Were all these lines joining up or were they just random scribbles?

When he'd digested the news, Harland said, 'By the way, those CCTV tapes have arrived from Bristol airport. You want to see them now?'

With a mounting sense that the case was beginning to gather impetus, he pushed himself out of his chair.

'What are we waiting for?'

He followed her to the incident room, settled down in a corner where a machine and a large screen had been set up. Harland selected a tape from her desk, slotted it into the machine. She sat down beside him, pushed the play button on the remote control and sighed theatrically.

'If only you were young and good-looking, sir, I could imagine I was on a date at the cinema instead of at work.'

He laughed. 'You'd never find me out with a female police officer, young lady. They get all the romance knocked out of them in this job. Didn't you know that?'

The first tape showed the students setting off from Bristol but there was nothing unusual there. The second tape was their flight arriving back. Davis spotted James moving through passport control with a girl by his side. He pointed to the figures on the screen.

'That's one of the lads. Looks like he's with a girl, doesn't it?'

James and the girl moved out of view. The tape ran on a little and Ted came through with another girl. Davis scratched his head as he pointed him out to Harland.

'The lads don't look as though they're together. They're both with ladies from the West Indies, aren't they?'

'Four days out there and they've picked up women,' Harland commented, raising an eyebrow. 'I'd call that pretty fast work.'

'What on earth's going on, Diane?'

Harland grinned. 'Well, they're not members of the constabulary and they're not old crusties. So romance isn't entirely out of it.'

'Two holiday romances?' Davis queried. 'I'm not sure even Cupid would go with those odds.'

Harland put in another tape, fast-forwarded to the baggage carousel. Davis spotted James first, then Ted.

'Look, they're standing on opposite sides of the carousel as though they're not with each other,' he said, perplexed. 'Have they rowed, or is it deliberate, do you think?'

On the next tape James and the girl walked through the customs channel first. Ted appeared quite a way behind, the girl leaning heavily on his shoulder. When she stumbled and fell, Davis sat forward. On the screen, people rushed to help the fallen girl and a crowd gathered. Ted was staring like a lost child, his face gaunt and anxious. A stretcher appeared on the scene. The bearers lifted the girl and carried her. Ted walked beside the stretcher like a zombie, a customs officer holding his elbow.

'By all the saints,' Davis exclaimed, his brain making great leaps. 'Could she be a drug mule and something burst in her stomach? That's happened before.'

'I suppose,' Harland commented. 'But it could be simply the effects of a long flight. Air sickness is a well known malady.'

He gave her a sharp glance. 'I saw the young man just yesterday so I'm probably wrong. Ring the customs people in Bristol for me when we've finished, find out the score.'

Reaching forward, she removed the tape, put another one in the machine.

'This is the last one,' she said. 'It shows another part of the channel.'

They watched the procession of passengers parading past on the screen.

'There!' Davis exclaimed, pointing to James and his girl.

They watched as James turned and looked back, the girl following suit. Obviously agitated, she started to go back but James's arm snaked out to restrain her. He whispered in her ear then marched her towards the exit.

'Masterful, isn't he,' Harland remarked.

'They saw the other girl go down,' Davis said. 'She wanted to go to her but he wouldn't allow it, even though his friend was back there. Why?'

'Now you're thinking drug-smuggling again.'

'It looks suspicious, doesn't it?'

'So I take it the holiday romances idea is stone dead?'

Davis grinned. 'With your imagination, you should write a novel.'

Harland rose from the chair, turned the tape off and stretched. 'Right, next thing, Bristol on the blower?'

'Soon as. I'll be back in my office waiting.'

With a bit of a spring in his step he returned to his office. He shuffled papers without absorbing much content because there was too much floating around his head. The perennial question was why would those lads, with their career prospects and an affluent lifestyle to look forward to, risk involvement in the drug scene. The other student, Hickson, had a different way with him, he thought, a harder edge underneath an outward affability. If there was something going on, where did he fit in? Why the trip to Trinidad? Diane's phone calls would, he hoped, enlighten him.

As soon as she entered his office he could tell from the downturn to her mouth, her laggardly movement, that she wasn't bringing much to the table that would please him.

'Out with it,' he said.

She tilted her head. 'False trail, I'm afraid. They examined the girl; found no drugs inside her, or in her luggage. She must have just been sick. They checked him out too, found nothing. She spent the night in hospital and was discharged the following day.'

Davis deflated. In spite of the warning he'd given himself, had he been too hopeful? He stared away into the far corner of the room, trying to work out his next move.

'Don't worry,' Harland said. 'You're used to these little diversions. You'll get a breakthrough.'

His eyes swivelled, bored right through her, as though he was looking beyond her, not really seeing.

'Diversions!'

'Sir?'

His eyes returned from that invisible horizon and he snapped back into himself.

'Diversions,' he repeated. 'You said diversions.'

'Did I?'

'The girl collapsing could have been staged to draw attention.'

Harland was quiet for a moment while she considered it. When she did speak, her tone was tentative.

'The other girl tried to go back to the stricken girl. If it was set up and she was carrying she wouldn't have.'

'He stopped her going back, Diane. Held her tight. Why?'

'You've got a valid point, sir. I'm just not sure.'

'Diane, I need you to—'

She anticipated him. 'To try to find out more about the girls.'

'Hope you don't know everything going on in my mind.'

'Don't know what you're going to do about those students?'

'Shock tactics, I think. Shake them up a bit. Make them believe I'm on to something. You know what young people are

DECEIVED

like when they're being harassed. Most of them come to the boiling-point pretty quick.'

She looked unconvinced 'You think you can pressure them into confessions?'

'Perhaps not, but they might try to cover their tracks if they think we're on to something. It'll stretch our resources but I'll arrange for them to be watched.'

'You really do think they're involved, don't you, sir?'

'Didn't suspect them at first, not at all. It's been a slow build-up. Little things in their behaviour.' He sighed. 'Can't see a motive. But then you can't always, can you? Guys with the world at their feet decide they want the universe. Lawyers aren't immune. Sharper than sharks' teeth when it comes to money, some of them.'

'My ex-boyfriend was a lawyer,' Harland said, moving to the door. 'He was the one before the computer jerk came along. He had false teeth, like you, sir. Used to have his own but I knocked out the front two when he cheated on me with a bottle-blonde.'

Davis laughed. 'Get out of here, girl, before I've no illusions left in my life.'

The door closed and Davis stretched. He was thinking sometimes tiddlers could lead you to the big fish.

Harland returned within half an hour. She'd worked fast. Customs at Bristol had informed her that the girl who'd collapsed had flown back to Trinidad two days later. The other girl didn't appear in any passenger lists. From that, they concluded she'd either flown out from another airport, or was still in the country.

As they walked out of the office, Davis said, 'When I was a kid I won a prize for building a sandcastle on Redcar beach. Cried my eyes out when the tide took it.'

She gave him a quizzical look. 'Ever the sentimentalist, sir. That's you.'

143

'You get it though, don't you?'

'You can only go with what you've got. Nobody can expect more.'

As he closed the door, he said. 'Only myself.'

26

DAVE HICKSON LAY back in the chair, felt the breeze on his face, hoped the fresh country air would improve the pasty look he'd acquired in hospital. He'd looked at himself in the mirror that morning, thought his appearance had improved; the swelling around his jawline was much reduced, only the faintest traces of bruising remained now. Why they'd sent him to a convalescent home, he couldn't figure. Perhaps, in their ignorance of his true state of mind, they thought a change of scenery would help him relax and that that would help him regain his memory.

He had to admit that Middleton-one-Row, a country village beside the River Tees, was an ideal setting for the old country house converted for the purpose. The extensive garden, in which he was sitting now, was an arboreal treat, full of nooks and crannies where you could find privacy. You could hear yourself think and the tranquillity had enabled him to form an idea to which he was giving serious consideration. Winston had granted him a reprieve but his time was running out. He would have to pay up soon. The problem was still the same, however: he just hadn't enough money. So what if he discharged himself, headed back to Leeds, left a false address? Winston wouldn't have a clue where he'd gone. It wasn't as though he had any reason to linger here on Teesside. Liz had made her choice; she was a lost cause. Memories and sentiment were excess baggage, not worth the time of day if you wanted to reach the top unencumbered. He closed his eyes, satisfied with his plan. In the big house someone was playing the piano and the notes drifted across the lawns, soporific and seductive. He found himself drifting away. First he'd return to Leeds, then maybe head to London – a big-time lawyer in the city….

'Lord Hickson of Middleton-one-Row in repose. How sweet!'

Hickson heard the words. For a moment, lost in his somnolence, he had no idea where the voice came from, thought it belonged in his dreams. Then he remembered where he was and opened his eyes, to find James and Ted standing over him, blocking out the sky.

'Hello boys,' he said, trying to sound welcoming. He pushed himself upright and gestured at two chairs. 'Surprised they let the scruff in here – and you're a bit early. Not time for tea and crumpets yet and the butler's indisposed.'

He watched them as they sat down. He knew them well enough to detect that they weren't at ease. For certain, they had something on their minds. It made him curious and not a little unnerved but he wasn't going to push it, would let them tell it in their own time.

'The hospital informed us they'd moved you here,' Ted opened. 'It's a cut above, isn't it?'

James shuffled in his seat and swept the gardens and house with his eyes. 'Very nice indeed.'

Hickson manufactured a smile. Such evasive politeness and small talk – but what did it portend?

'As nice as Trinidad, I presume?'

He'd gained an advantage there. They both gave him rigor mortis grins and it went quiet for a moment.

James said, 'We shouldn't have gone to Trinidad. Not when you were in hospital. Circumstances—'

Hickson cut him short. ''Course you should. You'd worked

hard, deserved it. I would have gone. Seize the day and everything else, I say.'

Back in the house a female started to sing, accompanied by the piano. The voice was strident, out of tune.

Ted coughed, cleared his throat. 'Actually, Trinidad wasn't our idea.'

Hickson felt a momentary panic. Did they suspect he'd sold them down the river? Surely not! If they'd found him out, they'd have been at his throat, not sitting there like two old grannies at a tea party. He affected a bemused expression.

'It was a present from Mummy and Daddy, was it? A reward for your efforts! Me, I'll be lucky to get a hamburger at Macdonald's!'

He didn't raise a smile. James was staring into the distance beyond the trees at the end of the garden where the River Tees snaked its way through the countryside.

'We've got something to confess,' he muttered. 'Something unpleasant. You might not like us very much when you hear it.'

Ted added, nervously. 'You might hate us.'

Hickson responded with a wry grin. They obviously felt they'd done him some disservice, not the other way round.

'You've won the lottery at last,' he said, feigning joviality, 'took advantage of my indisposition and didn't put my name on the ticket this time!'

Neither of them smiled. He saw Ted's anxious expression, watched him trail his hand to the side of the chair, pluck a flower from the flower-bed, roll the petals in his fingers, crushing them into little pieces.

Ted said, 'This is serious. It might help you regain your memory about – that night.'

Hickson adjusted his face, jovial to sombre. Confession time, then. He might have known they couldn't just forget it, live with what they'd done. If only they knew the truth.

'OK 'he said. 'If we have to be serious, I'm all ears.'

James sat forward, fingers intertwined. He told the tale, Ted chipping in occasionally with a mitigating comment. Hickson pretended shock as each critical detail emerged, horror when they battered Winston and again when they were taken to look at his coffin. The Trinidad business and the girl's appearance at the flat rounded off the story.

'My God,' he exclaimed at the finish. They were staring at him like prisoners in the dock waiting for the judge to pronounce a verdict, 'Murder and smuggling. I can't believe it.'

His flatmates looked agitated, older than their years. He couldn't help himself revelling in their predicament. The descent of their lives into chaos made him feel superior to them for once and he liked that. It was time they had their share of trouble.

'You must hate us,' Ted said. 'We delayed calling the ambulance and we left you alone in that alley. You – you could have died.'

Hickson allowed a dramatic pause, then said. 'I don't hate you. You did what you had to do to cover your backs. I'd have done the same. Besides, getting rid of those ecstasy tablets saved my bacon. To some extent, I owe you.'

He watched their faces, could see relief come flooding in, knew they were thinking how magnanimous he was being, and after they'd deceived him all this time. But why were they confessing now, he wondered? Was there something they hadn't said yet, something that had prompted this attempt to reconcile their consciences? He was sceptical enough of human nature to suspect that this was so. The girl and her drugs interested him too. Was all this something to do with that little scenario with her?

'So you've got the girl and the drugs in the flat and you don't know what to do. And those men might come back.'

'We thought it was over,' Ted groaned. 'But it's turning into another nightmare.'

Hickson nodded thoughtfully. He was pretty sure they must need his help, were just slow coming to the point.

'So what will you do?'

Like two dancers, uncertain who should lead off in case they entangled their feet, both hesitated. James took the initiative, poked out a tentative toe.

'We don't like to ask after all you've been through.'

'You need my help?' Hickson said, pretending surprise.

Ted overcame his inhibition, at last got to it. 'We know you bought drugs – small scale. We were wondering if you knew anyone who would take the drugs off our hands.'

'You want to give away drugs?'

'Not give away,' James came in. 'Just sell them cheap and give the girl the money to get her home, out of our hair.'

'How much are they worth, these drugs?'

'They told her fifty thousand.'

Hickson whistled long and low. His first thought was that there might be a way to gain a percentage for himself in this. It wouldn't be difficult for him to pass the word to the right people, people who'd jump at a sale. But in these matters there was always scope for things to go badly wrong. James and Ted were naïve and it was a bigger sum of money than he'd been used to handling. But he did know foot soldiers who had the ears of generals. Right now it might be best to play for time, refine details later with, of course, proper consideration for his own whack.

'Like you say, I've dabbled, spoken to people on the fringes. I could maybe put out feelers.'

Their faces lit up with gratitude. Poor mites! They were adrift in an ocean whose depths they couldn't conceive, so far from their cosseted existence that he could almost feel sorry for them. The best of it was they were looking to him to be their captain and saviour, the one who would bring them safely back to port. Where was that public-school confidence and *savoir faire* now when they needed it?

'If you could find someone, it might be a way out for the girl,' James said. 'Then we'd be done with the whole business too.'

Hickson shook his head. A half-smile, which he made no attempt to hide, played on his lips.

'What?' Ted grunted.

'Forgive me,' Hickson answered, 'I'm just thinking, you two are pretty cool dudes. You got away with murder, didn't you?'

'We're not proud of it,' James snapped, 'We did it to save you.' He softened his voice. 'You'll never tell anyone, will you?'

Hickson raised his arms, held out his hands, palms upward. 'The guy was a small-time drug dealer hitting on me for a loan. He was high and went wild when I refused him. I danced with the devil and got burned. You pulled me out of the fire. Why would I want to tell anybody?'

'That's good, then,' James said. 'And you will try to find us a buyer?'

'Sure! There's someone I can ring. Come back tomorrow and we'll see what I've got.'

They mumbled their thanks. For a while they tried to make small talk. But things had changed between them and the conversation was stilted, as though they had little in common any more.

James stood up and Ted followed his lead.

'We're grateful to you for taking it so well,' James said, 'and agreeing to help.'

Hickson tried to look suitably embarrassed. 'Hey, what are friends for? You'd do the same for me. Go and get some sleep, for heaven's sake. You look worse than you did during the final exams.'

He lay back in the chair, watched them walk away across the flawless green lawns. Putting his head back, he started to plan. Whom would he approach? Where could an exchange be made and how? There was also the important question of how much he was going to milk out of this without James and Ted finding out. He was well aware that he had to be careful. This was a dangerous business. Things could go badly wrong if you weren't clued up.

He considered it a pity Winston hadn't been dead in that coffin as his old pals believed. Only days ago, the gangster had visited him in James Cook Hospital in disguise, just to remind him the clock was running down on his debt. Perhaps, he had an opportunity now to manipulate a deal so that £10,000 came his way and afterwards to pay Winston his £5,000. Better still, maybe he could just forget Winston, keep it all for himself, cut and run for Leeds. Winston would be none the wiser and he'd have starter money for a new life. All he needed was the nerve to do it.

Five minutes later, dreaming up a new life, he heard a rustling sound in the nearby bushes, as though the wind had suddenly stirred itself to a greater effort. He opened his eyes. At the edge of his vision he caught a faint movement, realized someone was standing there watching him. His skin prickled and he jerked his head in that direction.

Winston was standing there, his face impassive. He held a flower in his big, gnarled hand, where it looked more incongruous than lipstick on a pugilist. Hickson's mouth dropped open. Struggling to believe what he was seeing, he swallowed hard, tried to recover his composure.

'You got it good here, man. Could even make a feller forget about things, huh?' Winston smiled sardonically as he spoke.

Hickson blurted out, 'Who told you I was here?'

Winston threw away the flower. 'I worry you forget me so I watch, follow your friends.'

'I'm not going anywhere. Where would I go?'

Winston shrugged. 'You got two weeks left. Don't be running home. You do – I follow you to Leeds, man. Wherever. I find you.'

Hickson's dreams melted away like grease off a candle. His disappointment showed in his face.

'I find out where you come from,' Winston continued, smiling at his own cleverness.

Hickson tried to get over it, to see the positive side. If he played the cards he'd been dealt, he would still be able to pay the brute off, have done with him once and for all and still show a profit.

Winston continued. 'You be on time with my money or it won't be nice.' He surveyed the gardens with a smirk. 'Maybe they make it permanent here next time. You understand.'

'I got it loud and clear.'

Winston plucked another flower. His face a picture of concentration, he tried to thread the stem through his buttonhole. It broke and he threw the flower away. He glanced at Hickson meaningfully.

'Useless thing, break too easy,' he said. 'But you got the message, so I'm done here.'

Thoughts had been sprinting through Hickson's head. There was never certainty that a drug deal would go down the way you wanted. With lowlifes there were too many variables, always someone wanting more than his share of the meat at the table. You could lose everything and he hated to think about that, the consequences for him. Needs must, then. This visit had changed things. No good denying it. He had to reverse his thinking, be adaptable. There was a way to cut his losses, go for certainties. As Winston was turning away, he called to him.

'No excuses,' Winston snapped, facing him again. 'You've run out. I ain't buying.'

Hickson hesitated, tried to foresee all angles, thought he had them covered.

'We can do a deal.'

Winston made a show of looking at his watch. 'Spit it out.'

Hickson started talking. When he'd finished, the black man's eyes lit up.

'Will that do it?' Hickson said.

Winston shook his head. 'You're a real piece of work, man.'

'Will it do?'

'It'll do it and more – if you ain't lying.'

27

'WHAT'S THE TIME?' James enquired as he turned the car into the street.

'Gone six already,' Ted told him.

James's stomach rumbled, which made him wonder whether it was down to his nervous state, or just indigestion from the heavy meal they'd eaten on the way back from the convalescent home. He glanced at his friend.

'Two and a half hours we've been away. Hope she's all right up in that loft.'

'I think she's glad of a haven,' Ted said. 'A place where she's safe for a while.'

'Sooner she's out of there the better,' James said. 'I won't sleep until she is. It's like having the sword of Damocles hanging over our heads. Wonder how long it'll take our old pal to fix something up?'

'Contact him tomorrow, that's what he said. Not too bad, considering what we've asked of him.'

James swung the car off the road into the drive, cut the engine. He leaned back in the seat, stared at the house, seemed reluctant to get out of the car.

'Tomorrow never comes,' he mumbled, eyes fixed ahead, as though he was seeing the future and it looked bleak.

Ted gave him a sharp look. 'What's that meant to mean? We're still in the game, you know.'

James rubbed a hand over his face, reached for the ignition key.

'Just an old film title, I think. It jumped into my mind. Seemed appropriate somehow. During this whole stinking business we've kept looking for a better day.' He sighed. 'Wish we could turn back the clock, do things differently.'

'If we're on films, try to think more on the lines of *Back to the Future*,' Ted commented. 'Like we're taking a few backward steps to secure the future.'

'I thought I was the optimistic one,' James stated. He made an effort to perk himself up. 'But you're right, of course. We're not done for yet.'

He reached for the handle, opened the door, paused a moment. 'Sorry about that. Just a mood. Maybe Hickson really will come up trumps tomorrow.'

'I'll drink to that,' Ted said and climbed out of the car. They glanced at the house.

'Poor girl,' Ted said. 'A stranger in a foreign land, nowhere to go and only us to help her.'

James put the key in the door, turned it. Before he pushed it open he said, 'Don't get too sensitive about her. We can help her but, if needs be, we have to put ourselves first.'

'Our original mistake,' Ted commented wryly. 'The original sin.'

James entered and Ted followed. James started to say something but his words tumbled back down his throat. Two black men had emerged from the kitchen and were pointing guns at them. Neither of the intruders said a word, didn't need to. The guns and the menace evident in their faces said it all for them. One false move and they'd use their weapons. The students reeled back, froze. Thoughts raced through James's head. Could they be burglars? If so, all they had to do was stand aside, let them leave. But he knew it was rare for burglars to carry guns. Had they been looking for the girl?

One of the men waved his gun towards the living-room door. James, reluctant to move, felt as though his feet were encased in concrete blocks but he dragged them along the hall to the room. Ted followed him, breathing like an old steam train as he fought to contain his terror. As they passed the door to the spare room they noticed it had been smashed in and their hearts sank.

The girl was in the middle of the living room, tied to a chair, her back towards the door. The man was standing over her holding a knife. His eyes bored into the flatmates. There was not a fraction of humanity in those eyes, just a depth of blackness where it seemed impossible for anything but evil to reside. James's gaze moved to the gun in his belt. It was fitted with a long silencer. Perspiration burst on to his forehead. His heart banged against his chest and desert heat enveloped him As though seeking to escape the confines of his beleaguered body, blood surged to the surface of his skin. Body and mind were warning him that, dangerous as this man had been during their previous encounter, this time was different. This time there was a coldness about him that seemed to emanate from the core of his being, filter out to the air around him. James sensed it was the enemy of anything that possessed the precious gift of life.

'My name's Bradley,' he said, drawing back his arm. 'Since we're getting so cosy you might as well know that.'

In a blur of movement, he slashed the girl's face. Her scream was a drawn-out agony which died away into heavy sobs. Her shoulders started to jerk as spasms of pain hit her. The students stared at each other, horror and shame intermingling.

Bradley wiped the blade between finger and thumb, then licked the girl's blood from his finger as though it was a delicacy to be savoured. He dragged the flat of the blade across the front of the girl's blouse to clean it. Fearing a repeat performance, she let out another scream, shrank as far away from him as her restraints would allow.

Bradley's eyes flickered towards the students. 'She lie to me. She say she don't know where the drugs are. She take for me a fool.'

James stammered. 'You ... didn't have to do that. She doesn't know.'

The eyes came back, two fuses just waiting to be lit. 'Better tell, boy, if you know.' He pointed the knife. 'Or I decorate this place with blood.'

James, his mind adrift in a sea of fear, tried to think of a way out. He was stuck between a rock and a hard place. If they gave him the drugs, this creature could decide to kill them for betraying him. If they didn't give them up, he was likely to butcher them slowly to make them tell. One look at his friend told him Ted understood the dilemma, was looking to him. He made his decision. Giving the man his drugs might placate him enough for him to let them live.

'They're in the boot of the car.'

Bradley nodded contemptuously. 'Amateurs,' he said, gesturing to one of his men who stepped in front of James. 'Best you not be lying. Give my man there the keys and we see.'

Barely able to control his shaking fingers, James felt inside his pocket for the keys and handed them over. The henchman grabbed them and left the room.

Except for the girl's sobs, they waited in silence for him to return. Intending to offer her a little comfort, James made a move towards her but the other gangster pulled him away. Bradley was looking agitated. James thought it was a distinct possibility that he needed a fix and the idea terrified him because the man was already unpredictable.

The henchman returned with a hold-all, laid it at Bradley's feet, bent down on one knee and unzipped it. He extracted one of the small bags and looked up at his boss. Bradley handed him the knife, watched as he slit the bag open and tasted the powder. Grinning, he looked up.

'That's the real bitch,' he said. 'You can take her home to Daddy any time.'

A beatific look adorned Bradley's face. As though he was about to go into rapture, he shut his eyes and breathed deeply. James dared to hope, now that the gangster was happy, that there was at least a chance he'd let them alone. But when Bradley opened his eyes, the devil was back in them. He reached for the gun in his belt, drew it and stepped right up to the girl. She looked up at him, ceased her sobbing and whimpered like a puppy as he placed the silencer against her temple. In the magnitude of that moment, time seemed to stop and wait.

The sound was no more than a soft sibilance, the gentlest of coughs. A jet of blood spurted from the girl's head, just missed Ted. Her shoulders sagged and her head lolled forward.

Ted cried out in shock, 'Oh God!'

Stunned, James stared at the girl's lifeless body. His mind refused to focus. Only the urge for self-preservation was strong enough to keep him on his feet and functioning. When his mind came back to him, he was conscious that Bradley had hold of Ted's arm. The gun was still in his hand. He saw Ted try to pull back only to be pushed forward again by one of the men behind him. In that same moment, James was enveloped by strong arms.

Ted started to struggle but a flurry of blows drove him to his knees. His face was white, drained of blood like a corpse on a mortuary slab. Bradley put the gun against his head. Disbelieving, James heard himself scream like a banshee. In a frenzy, he tried to break away from those arms holding him, but to no avail. The gangster's gun coughed a second time and blood and brains sprayed outwards. Ted's body went slack, tottered, then toppled forward and hit the floor with a thump. His neck was twisted at an awkward angle and his dead eyes looked up at James as though in amazement.

Rooted to the spot, James stared at his dead friend. He couldn't comprehend what had happened, the suddenness and finality of his friend's death. Part of his mind refused to accept it, believed that at any moment life would return to animate those lifeless eyes.

From the corner of his eye, he saw Bradley raise the gun again. He dragged his eyes from his friend, stared at the barrel, accepting. What was the use of struggling? What was the point in trying to avoid the inevitable? Ted had gone. The world was crazy. Better to leave the madhouse for a place where there would be no more pain to endure.

28

DC HARLAND PREPARED herself for a spell of real tedium. She had relieved another detective, more a rookie than she was herself, so that he could nip off and have something to eat. She hated this kind of thing. It was only one step up from watching paint dry, so thank goodness it would only be for an hour. A longer spell of mental and physical inertia would drive her up the wall. Nothing was going to happen, she was sure. This was a quiet street, hardly any traffic. The flat belonged to students and they would surely have enough grey matter to know that, if there was dirty work to be done, it was best kept well away from home ground.

A Mercedes entering the road caught her eye. Instinctively she lowered herself in the seat so that her eyes were level with the steering-wheel. She watched the vehicle draw up to the kerb opposite the flat. Three black men, all with powerful physiques, got out of the car. The wind caught a jacket, lifted a flap, gave her a fleeting glimpse of a gun stuck in a waistband. The owner immediately slapped the jacket down and looked around. When he stared in her direction, she shrank further into the seat, her lethargy gone, senses activated.

She waited a few seconds, then risked another look. The muscle-men with their rolling gaits were crossing the road and entering the garden of the flat she was watching. One of them started on the lock while the other two tried to hide him with their bulk and checked out the street. The guy working on the lock was good, didn't take more than a few seconds. He pushed the door open, held it for his companions to step inside and followed them in, closing the door behind him.

Reanimated, Harland didn't bother with the car radio. Instead she called Harry Davis directly on her mobile. He answered straight away and, without a pause for breath, she gave him the story. He listened without interrupting, but when he did speak his voice was as enthusiastic as her own had been.

'Stay in the car and watch, Diane. I'll have the road sealed off and the armed response unit on the way in no time.'

She voiced her concern. 'What if something happens before they get here?'

'Stay in the car,' he repeated. 'Don't go in. Too dangerous.'

As soon as she had confirmed that she understood he cut her off.

Harland was another person now, edgy for action. Moments ago this street had looked like any other. It still did, outwardly. But everything had changed. The gun had done that. The street's ordinariness was now a mere façade; behind one of its doors was a potential powder keg. Would someone light the fuse, she wondered?

Minutes ticked by. Her eyes were everywhere. But nothing was happening and she forced herself to calm down, be patient. At last she noticed signs of movement way up the street. Two men came into view, walking briskly. She watched them split up, each take a side of the road and knock on doors. They were obviously plainclothes police sent to warn the occupants to stay out of sight. At last it was beginning. She sighed her relief because the men were still inside; the trap would be closing in. The armed response unit wouldn't be far away, was likely moving into position.

When there was another movement further up the road her eyes leapt to it. A car was coming into the street. She supposed it could be an unmarked police car, failing that a vehicle that had slipped through just before the road was sealed. She expected it to drive past, be long gone before the action began. But instead it decelerated as it came nearer to the house. Fists clenched on the steering wheel, she sat forward.

The worst thing happened: the car parked in front of the target house. Harland let go a string of imprecations. This was bad. To make it worse, she recognized the two students getting out. As they started up the drive, she gripped the door handle, thinking she should get out and stop them. But they were suspected of colluding with the gangsters. If she interfered, she might blow the whole operation. Davis's instruction was to stay in the car, but he hadn't allowed for this contingency. Judging by the distance she'd have to cover, the fact that one of them was already putting the key in the lock, she realized she wouldn't make it anyway. Hoping she wasn't watching innocent lambs entering a slaughterhouse, she let it go.

She reached for her mobile, intending to ring Davis, let him know the new factor in the equation. Before she pressed the numbers, she caught a movement in the driver's mirror. She realized it was Davis approaching on foot.

Smiling like the cat who got the cream, her boss slipped into the back seat. She opened her mouth to explain what had just happened but he cut her off.

'The snipers are in position. The mobile will drive up in a moment and we'll start this thing.'

She pointed to the student's car, told him about the latest arrivals, wondering whether it would change things; not least, curb the enthusiasm she had heard in his voice.

He didn't take it too badly. After a pause, he said. 'My bet is they're involved. Anyway, we have to play it out now, go in mob-handed if necessary. You saw a gun so those are dangerous men.'

29

'NOBODY DISSES ME!'

James heard Bradley say the words, felt the gun barrel pressing against his forehead. He closed his eyes, accepted what was happening. Another second and he'd be following his friend into oblivion, either that or a better world. Death came to everyone and this was his moment. His main regret was his parents were losing their only son.

'Inside the house! Can you hear me!'

The voice, slightly distorted, filtered through to him as though from a great distance and, bizarrely, seemed like a voice from another world calling to him. Much nearer, he heard another voice.

'What the devil…?'

The second voice, as cold and unremitting as an icy Arctic blizzard, he recognized as Bradley's.

He felt the gun move off his forehead. Opening his eyes, he saw Bradley had moved to the window. One of the other men stepped over Ted's body, slipping in blood as he rushed to join his boss. James was struggling to come to terms with the fact that he was still alive, but gradually a burning rage sprang to life inside him like a phoenix rising from the ashes. His blood surged to the beat of its wings. Passive acceptance gave way to a growing fury at these beasts of men, and at himself for the mistakes he'd made that had led to this carnage.

His eyes were wide-open when the distant voice came again. He realized that someone out in the street was using a loudhailer.

'This is Detective Inspector Davis. We have the house surrounded. Everyone in the house step outside, one at a time. Keep your hands in the air.'

Bradley, lips drawn back, teeth bared like a wild dog's, kicked out at a lampstand, sent it sprawling. He followed that with a torrent of curses which made clear what he thought of the police and what they could do to themselves if he didn't get there first. He was the bandleader and his men danced to his tune, making angry gestures with their arms and repeating their leader's curses.

'What we do now, man?' one of them asked when the cursing ceased. His voice was high-pitched, a hint of desperation there.

The other gangster pulled out his gun. His eyes were bulging, as though at any moment they could jump from their sockets. It lent him an insane look.

Bradley's eyes were everywhere, his neck swivelling and stretching like a demented cockerel's. They came to rest on James. In two giant strides, he crossed the room, grabbed him by the collar. Looking pleased with himself, he turned to the others.

'This one our ticket out.'

His men brightened, became calmer; Bradley had found a way to salvation.

One of them stared at the floor, shook his head, 'But how they find us here, man? Somebody grass?'

'No time for that now, fool,' Bradley snapped. 'You throw those bodies out, let them see we ain't messing with them. After, you pick up the drugs.'

James managed to contain his mounting fury. He was determined to do something, but he had to choose his moment and this wasn't it. Sickened, he watched the men dragging the bodies out of the room as though they were pieces of meat fresh from the slaughterhouse. When they returned, one of them stooped and picked up the hold-all containing the drugs.

Bradley pressed the gun barrel into James's neck, pushed him into the hall. The gangster's other hand gripped his collar so tight it wasn't easy to breathe. When they reached the front door he forced his face against the wall.

'Watch him!' he told one of the men, then let his collar go and removed the gun barrel.

James heard the door open and Bradley's voice shouting.

'We got a live one here. You try stopping us, he die like the others.'

'You tell them, Bradley,' one of the gangsters whooped.

In spite of the gansters' ebullience there was tension in the hallway. James could feel it growing by the second until the hall seemed too small to contain it. Something would have to happen, and soon, or it would explode.

'They not buying,' one of the henchmen said.

The other one said. 'They think we bluffing. Who they think we are, man? Kindergarten kids.'

Bradley came close to James. He heard the man's breathing accelerate like a predator's as it builds its momentum to the point when it unleashes its full ferocity. It was barely under control as he gave his orders.

'We not wait. We go out together.'

He pushed James to the door. One arm snaked round his neck, the muscular forearm pressing against his windpipe in a stranglehold. With the other hand he held the gun against James's head once again.

'You seen them siege movies,' he grunted, twisting the barrel like a corkscrew. 'Well, this ain't the movies. This time the bad guys win. You be good or it be your blood on the path.'

James said nothing, showed not a flicker of emotion, but he was near boiling point. One opportunity was all he asked. Then he'd have his revenge for what these barbarians had done. It wouldn't matter if he died in the process because his life was finished now. His friend was dead. Whatever integrity or honour he'd naïvely believed himself to possess was in pieces, had been destroyed when Ted and the girl were shot. He was a worthless nothing. Retribution was all he had left.

Bradley edged the door open. Holding James in front of him, he stepped on to the threshold. A bird perched in a nearby tree was chirping merrily, the sound surreal. What right did it have to be happy when there were bodies a few feet away? James squinted at the corpses spread-eagled on the path. Ted's eyes were open and staring up at him.

'Stop right there!'

The order seemed to come down from an omniscient god in the sky above. But it had an earthly source. James could see the man who had issued it standing in the street holding a megaphone. Bradley ignored his command and with a curse pushed James ahead of him.

'Try to stop us, this boy dies,' he yelled.

The man with the megaphone disappeared behind a van. Everything went quiet. The bird stopped singing, winged its way across the street and landed on the roof of the house opposite. Other birds joined it there and they seemed to be watching like harbingers in black funeral attire, as though by some collective prescience they knew something was about to happen.

Bradley pushed James again. As they moved forward, one of the men started to panic.

'It too quiet, man. They planning to kill us.'

'They won't risk it,' the other one said but didn't sound too sure.

Bradley's arm squeezed tighter against James's windpipe.

James was aware how easily, with sheer brute strength, the gangster could snuff out his life. Would he die before he got the chance he was waiting for?

Bradley, sensing his men's hesitancy, hissed contemptuously.

'You pussy cats stay if you want. Jail ain't my party. Make up your mind what you do.'

One of them answered, 'We with you, man. Got to take chances.'

Bradley grunted. 'You got it.'

The gangster kept forcing James ahead. The arm round his throat was so tight he felt like a small, helpless animal dragged by a powerful lion. Halfway down the path he had a better view of the police vehicles blocking the road, noticed heads peering from behind them, watching their progress.

The voice came over the megaphone once again. 'That's far enough. Stop there so we can talk.'

Bradley laughed insanely. Over his shoulder he scoffed, 'They not shoot – scared they hit the boy – or we kill him. Scared of what the papers say.'

They reached the pavement and the watchers had made no move. Only the width of the road lay ahead now. Once they crossed, they'd be at the car. James was desperate for a chance, couldn't see how he was going to get one. If they got away, he was sure they'd put a bullet in his head and that would be it.

Bradley forced him on to the road. The gangsters bunched as close as sheep in a huddle. Now they were totally exposed to snipers waiting for the command to take them down and, in spite of Bradley's boast, they couldn't be sure the command wouldn't be given.

Bradley was still pressing the gun against his head and maintaining his stranglehold when they reached the car. He pushed James against the door, held him there like a wrestler trapping his opponent against the ropes.

'The keys,' one of the men said. His voice rose a pitch. 'Who's got the keys, damn it?'

Three pairs of eyes met, each wondering, each doubting.

Bradley ended it. 'I got them.'

He must have believed the gun against James's head would be sufficient inhibition because he released his grip on James's neck and started to reach for his inside pocket. James gulped air, aware this was a chance; not much of one, possibly his last. Suppressed anger roared through his system, fuelled his adrenaline. Palms flat, he pushed against the car with all his strength, simultaneously thrust his head backwards. The back of his skull smashed into the gangster's face and the noise of bones cracking told him he had done damage. With a feeling of exhilaration he spun round, wanting more of the same. Bradley staggered back, holding a bloodied and broken nose. He still had the gun but his eyes were glazed as though he didn't know where he was. The other gangsters were staring wide-eyed at their leader, as though seeing him as a vulnerable mortal for the first time, unable to comprehend it.

James focused only on Bradley. He lowered his shoulders and charged at his midriff harder than he had ever driven into any rugby scrum, determined to put his man down and beat him to pulp. As he cannoned into the gangster's stomach, in the distance he heard sounds like bones cracking but he didn't let it divert him from his purpose.

Bradley went down surprisingly easily for a man of such bulk. James fell on top of him, pounded him with his fists, all his hate channelled into the blows. He was beyond any rational thought now. In his singular state of mind he didn't wonder why Bradley wasn't fighting back, why there was a red flower of blood blooming in the centre of the gangster's forehead, nor was he aware that the other two gangsters had gone down.

Strong arms grabbed him from behind, hauled him off. He

fought against them, cursed those attempting to restrain him, tried to resume his onslaught. Slowly the rage subsided and he emerged from the dark tunnel. The world around him took shape again. He saw the blood and the bullet holes, realized that the three gangsters on the ground were beyond his vengeance, were as dead as he considered his own soul to be. Then everything came back to him, pummelled his brain with renewed force and his body started to convulse. Those arms held him more tightly, guided him away from the scene. Someone threw a blanket over his shoulders. Soothing voices were trying to calm him. His feet started to move of their own volition. He was aware of going up steps, entering an ambulance. Other arms guided him on to a bed. He felt the sharp prick of a needle and, as they laid him down, he was aware of a flashing blue light and a whining sound like the dogs of Hell unleashed. It all faded away as blackness slipped over his body like a warm glove, carried him away from a reality that was too much to bear.

30

THE WALLS WERE grey, that same dirty grey as clouds before a storm. If there was a staging post for Hell, a preparation for initiates, James figured this room would qualify. He'd recognized the policeman sitting on the opposite side of the desk but not the young woman with him who had introduced herself as Detective Constable Harland. Right now they were staring at him as though they wanted more from him. He lowered his head, studied the palm of his hand, imagined himself a fortune teller trying to interpret the preordained events supposed to be there in the lines, waiting to be deciphered. Had his fate been preordained, he wondered, or had it all been just down to weak character?

After that horrific day when Ted had died, he'd confessed everything and they'd put him in prison on remand. It had been six weeks now and the numbness that had come on the day of the killings had never left him entirely. Even when his parents had visited him he'd withdrawn from them, refused to talk, told them he was sorry he'd let them down but he didn't want them to visit him again, would refuse to see them because he wasn't worthy of them. He'd refused legal help; he was prepared to accept whatever the courts threw at him. Now, for some reason that he couldn't fathom, these two detectives had come to see him and asked him to repeat his story. A fellow prisoner, pretending wisdom, had told him the truth would set him free. Well, he didn't feel any better going over it all again. How could he? The feeling of shame was with him every day.

'And that's it?' Davis said, shutting off the tape recorder.

James raised his eyes. 'That's it.'

He wondered how two little words could encompass so much pain, précis so much heartbreak, convey such finality too. Davis and Harland stared at him doubtfully.

Davis said, 'So Dave Hickson was beaten up for no reason that you are aware of and that was the catalyst that set it all off. Other than that, he wasn't involved?'

James nodded his head curtly. He hadn't told them about Hickson's drug dealing, nor that he'd approached him about setting up a drug deal hours before all hell had broken loose. He'd been tempted, but decided it would just ruin another life when enough damage had been done. The burden of guilt was his. If he'd taken different decisions Ted and the girl would be alive. He deserved punishing. Deflecting blame would be another weak act on his part. Facing the truth about himself, taking whatever was coming to him, was the only way to salvage a vestige of decency. The truth might set you free but you didn't have to drag everyone down with you.

'That's the story you'll be telling in court?' Harland queried, a hint of sympathy in her tone and in the softening in her eyes.

'Yes.'

Davis shook his head. 'It won't hold up, son.'

James shrugged. He'd told them the important facts. Why were they trying to drag this out? What more did they want out of him? He had nothing left to say.

Davis wouldn't let it go, though. 'All your actions,' he mused, 'rightly or wrongly, sprang from the fact that you'd murdered Winston Smart the night he attacked Hickson. From then on in, everything you did was an attempt to hide your crime because cousin Bradley threatened to expose you if you didn't co-operate.'

James didn't answer. He'd been clear enough. All he wanted to do was go back to the prison hospital. He needed to sleep. Reliving the stuff of his nightmares had drained him. The prison hospital was a depressing place where he was surrounded by criminals who had committed all kinds of heinous crimes. With time to reflect about what they'd done, some turned to religion with a mania, others turned into zombies. James worried about his sanity, found he needed constant sleep to replenish the energy drained from him by the weight of his guilt. Someone once told him Hell was in your mind and he was finding the truth of that statement all right.

'The reason it won't hold,' Harland said, breaking into the silence, 'is that Winston is very much alive. During the course of our enquiries we've found witnesses who saw him in the flesh long after you thought you'd murdered him.'

James's brain couldn't fully comprehend this. Was it some kind of cruel trick? He'd seen the man in his coffin. Dead men didn't rise?

'I guess Winston and Bradley could have set you up,' Davis continued. 'You could use that as mitigation. But ask yourself how the jury will see it. Your whole story sounds too far-fetched. You were supposed to be intelligent, a future lawyer in fact. How could anyone with brains fall for it, they'll wonder. Even if you did, why wouldn't you take it to the police? Won't they think you've just fabricated the whole tale in an attempt to conceal the fact that you were involved up to your eyes with those drug dealers?'

'Drugs were found beside the dead gangsters,' Harland chipped in. 'The prosecution will say you were doing a deal and it went wrong. They'll argue that's why your friends were killed and you were used as a hostage.'

James didn't want to hear any more. He fixed his eyes on a corner of the room where a spider was clinging to a gossamer line. In his mind he heard laughter, ironic laughter at his expense because he'd been so naïve. If they'd gone to the police in the first place Ted wouldn't have died. The waste brought tears streaming down his cheeks.

'We just want to make sure you've given us it all, son,' Davis said, not unsympathetically, 'so that justice is done, so that if, after the trial, you're sitting in a prison cell recalling this interview, you'll have no regrets.'

Up in the corner of the room the spider made a dart along the gossamer thread, engulfed a fly caught in its web. James felt a sudden, almost overwhelming sadness for the fly, one second going about its little bit of living, the next gone for ever. He dragged his eyes back to the detectives.

'I've told you everything you need to know,' he mumbled.

Davis blew out his cheeks. With a resigned expression he leaned back in his chair. There was silence for a moment, then he stood up, walked to the door, opened it and called to an officer waiting outside.

'We're done with him,' he said, his tone flat.

Without waiting to be told, James rose and walked to the door. He just wanted to get out of there. The visit had made him feel worse. He remembered that Ted's first reaction had been to call the police, that it was he who had had suggested the cover-up. Davis had spoken to him of regret. What did he know? Whatever length of sentence the court imposed, he deserved it.

As the door was closing, he heard Davis call out. 'You can always let us know if you've more to say. But if I were you I'd get the best lawyer I could.'

When James left the room Davis sat down again, shook his head. Harland sat with her hands in her lap, fingers interlocked, thumbs twiddling as she waited for him to speak. She couldn't figure her boss out. This case had more or less been put to bed. The Yardie threat had been excised. His superiors were pleased and he'd gained much kudos. Yet, right now, he was sitting there in a sullen silence looking dissatisfied with life.

She leaned towards him, elbowed him playfully in the ribs.

'Cheer up, sir! It's all down to you, you know, following hunches like an old sniffer hound that won't abandon the scent. You seemed to sense those students were involved.'

He pulled a face. 'Sniffer hound, eh! Now I know how you see me – big nose, big ears. Enough to bring on a mid-life crisis in a sensitive bloke like me.'

She smiled, pleased to see his sense of humour reviving.

'Ask me, sir, there's something getting up that big nose right now.'

Davis sighed. 'I think that young man was inveigled into it just as he says. Doesn't excuse him, but you can see how it could happen, how they found a weakness. Those bastards got to him, Diane.'

'You believe his story about the coffin?'

'Don't you?'

'Not sure. Sounds far-fetched, just as you said.' She pursed her lips. 'Maybe we'll never know, sir.'

'Winston Smart might confess, if we ever find him.'

'But why would he? Why would he give himself more grief?'

Davis ran a hand across his face. 'You're probably right. That young man's fate will be down to whether the jury believe him or not.'

She gave him a look which seemed wiser than her years. 'Who was it told me not to get emotionally involved? He has a lot to answer for, you know.'

Davis stared into her eyes. 'But he does deserve justice and it's up to us to do our best to see he gets it, even if he isn't helping himself. That apart, there are other aspects of the case which don't sit well with me.'

'You mean the other student – Hickson?'

'Yes! I don't think he was beaten up for nothing. I think our man James knows why but, for some reason, isn't telling.'

Harland leaned an elbow on the table, used the heel of her hand to prop up her jaw.

'Misguided loyalty to a friend perhaps?'

Davis shrugged. 'Several times I asked him why he thought Hickson was beaten up. He was dismissive, didn't want to speculate. When you consider what it led to, you'd expect a flicker of interest. I got the impression he wanted to get off the subject quickly.'

'Could be he genuinely doesn't know. Ask me, he isn't far from the edge and it's taking him all his time to concentrate on anything for long.'

Davis made no comment. He stood up, began to pace the room. Harland remained seated, saying nothing, allowing him time to think.

'Maybe he doesn't know,' he conceded at last. 'But I'm not convinced. Something's not right about Hickson. I've sensed it from day one, felt it in my bones every time I interviewed him. He's too streetwise, that one.'

'Forget it, sir. Take credit for what you've done. If James Harper won't speak the truth for his own sake, why should you worry?'

He shot her a look that could kill. 'It's not about credit. It's about the truth. I thought you knew that.' He softened his expression. 'I've a son about that age. Hate to think he got in a mess and had nobody to help him.'

Harland felt his rebuke but managed a smile. 'We'll just have to hope this Winston turns up somewhere and can be persuaded to talk.'

There wasn't much else to say. They'd hit a dead end and there was no point in lingering any longer in that bleak room. Harland unplugged the tape recorder, Davis carried it. Following behind, she closed the door a little too hard. The bang it made echoed in the corridor like a gunshot.

31

THE SUN SQUEEZED its way through the narrow barred window. A shaft of sunlight fell on James's pillow and on one side of his face. Like the touch of comforting fingers, he felt its warmth and opened his eyes thinking, for a moment, that he was a child again in his old bedroom, that it had been his mother's touch which had awakened him. Reality soon reasserted itself, disabused him of that notion. He allowed his eyes to wander. Near the barred window was a small basin with a cabinet above it where he kept his toiletries. Alongside the basin, squashed tight against it, was a narrow desk. High up in the corner a small television was fixed to the wall. Those sparse furnishings didn't bother him, nor did the hard bed on which he lay. He accepted the contrast to the comforts of former life because he felt he deserved the privations.

After his trial and sentencing, because his mind had been in a dark place, they'd kept him in the prison hospital for months. The temptation to end his life had been a stalking shadow. With the help of medication, a kind doctor and a priest of enduring patience, he'd come through the worst and entered the main part of the prison in a state of acceptance. Yet the spectre would still return, insisting he had no right to live when his friend was dead. Routine, keeping busy and taking every chance to exercise, were his weapons against it.

This morning he could feel the spectre closing in. Following his usual morning ritual, he slid off the bed, began his push-ups. But there was a lethargy in his efforts and he managed only fifty instead of his usual hundred. The spectre was hovering, telling him to raise the portcullis and let it in. What was the point of resisting its overtures? In the end, he'd surrender. It was just a matter of time.

He stood up, fixed his gaze on the crucifix hanging on the wall above his desk. The kind priest had talked to him of redemption, insisted no soul was beyond the reach of a loving God. He'd clung to that notion like a frightened child clings to its father's hand, repeated it like a mantra when the temptation was at its strongest and his body trembled with the weight of his conscience, or when Ted's face swam up from nowhere. He crossed himself and shut his eyes, hoping the dark presence would leave.

From the distance came the sound of feet echoing on hard floors, keys jangling. The screws were opening doors to herald another day filled with brain-deadening, monotonous routine, the struggle to prevent the wolves around you sniffing out your weaknesses. End it all, the spectre told him. You have the means. Temptation spiralled in his gut. He leaned over pulled at the loose stitching on his duvet, slipped his trembling fingers inside and extracted a small bundle of cotton wool. He opened it up and the sun's rays caught the fragment of broken glass which sparkled like a precious jewel. He stared at it like a miser at his most prized possession. Its attraction for him lay in its ability to end his misery. One slash and he'd be on his way out of the cruel world, to oblivion or, if that priest was right, to a better life where his torments would cease.

He lowered himself on to the bed, sat there thinking about Liz and the life he might have had with her. It had been a shock when he'd heard she'd married Hickson but he'd got over it. What he couldn't get over was the fact that neither of them had visited him. Liz, he could just about excuse, but Hickson was a bigger disappointment because he'd been part of it all. Sometimes, when he remembered that Hickson had known the girl was in the flat on that fateful day, he wondered about him. But it was just too much to believe that Hickson had anything to do with what happened. Only the lowest creature that crawled the earth could have betrayed her whereabouts, knowing what the bloody consequences were likely to be.

The sun moved away from the window. The room became darker and colder. The piece of glass lost its sparkle. He picked it up, held it between finger and thumb. One slash, that voice inside his head insisted, just one. He shoved the sharp edge against his veins. When he hesitated, the voice came again, rasping the accusation that he was a coward.

He felt too weak to resist any longer. What was the point? He gritted his teeth, was on the point of cutting the skin, when a noise like a clap of thunder made his body jerk back in surprise. A key started to turn in the lock and he realized that a screw had banged on the door. Hands shaking, he hurried to put the glass back in the duvet before he was discovered.

He just made it in time. A small, mean-mouthed screw stepped into the cell. His eyes roamed around before settling on James who was trying to come to terms with his ill-timed interruption.

'You got visitors, Harper,' the screw said in a sarcastic tone. 'They must be early birds looking for worms, eh! Not a worm, are you, Harper?'

James frowned. He rarely had visitors, had told his parents never to come, and this wasn't visiting hours. Another minute and his only visitors would have been angels – or devils. He stared wide-eyed at the screw who noticed his bemused expression.

'You're not on drugs, are you, sunshine? These visitors wouldn't like that one bit.'

James shook his head, pushed himself off the bed. He ran his fingers through his unruly hair, patted down his beard.

His voice was desiccated. 'What visitors?'

The screw smirked. 'Police! A man and a woman, so get dressed and get your act together. We don't want them thinking standards here are lower than in your average loony bin.'

James pulled on his shirt and pants, stepped into his shoes. What the hell could the police want with him and at this hour? They'd finished with him a long time ago.

'I'm ready,' he told the screw, with an air of weary resignation.

They stepped out of the cell and made their way out of the block, the screw constantly locking and unlocking doors. Once outside, they crossed a courtyard and entered another block. More doors were negotiated and at last the screw led him through a corridor and stopped outside one of the rooms. He knocked on the door and stepped inside.

'The prisoner, Harper,' James heard him say. 'I'll wait outside until you're done.'

32

THE ROOM JAMES stepped into was functional, but palatial compared to the rest of the prison. In the centre three armchairs were drawn up in a circle. Two were occupied and James recognized the occupants immediately.

He had learned to read faces in prison and detected a moment's doubt in Davis's and Harland's, knew it must be because of the beard and weight loss, not to mention the long hair. Their exchanged glance was fleeting but he saw they were pitying him.

Davis gestured at the unoccupied chair. 'Please sit.'

James obeyed, settled back, sank into its softness. He was feeling off centre, other worldly. Moments ago he'd been one step from eternity, so his presence in this room, facing these two detectives, seemed unreal, blurred at the edges, as though he'd been anaesthetized.

'How are you?' Harland opened, smiling at him pleasantly enough.

'Doing my time,' he answered, sharply. 'But, like I told you on our last meeting, I can't say I didn't do the crime, so I can't complain.'

Harland dropped her eyes. She'd detected the peevishness in his tone. What did he care? She'd asked a daft question. How did she think he was? Niceties didn't belong here. They were for another life in the polite society where he'd once belonged.

Davis cocked an eyebrow. 'We think you may be doing too much time, son. We think maybe it should be reduced.'

James's upper lip curled into a sneer. 'In this hole, Inspector, hope keeps some going, others it destroys when it disappoints. Me? I just drive along in neutral. If my sentence is cut, what's out there for me now anyway?'

Davis was quiet for a moment before he came back at him. 'But you would like to see justice done, wouldn't you? For your dead pal's sake, if not your own.'

James's eyes narrowed. Davis was a crafty one, knew Ted was his weak spot.

'Say what you've got to say, Inspector.'

'Remember Winston Smart?' Davis said, narrowing his eyes. 'The jury didn't believe your story about him and his coffin fetish, did they? They believed you and your mate Ted were involved in smuggling, that after it all blew up in your face you made up a story.'

'I told the truth. But what does that matter? It's old ground.'

Davis sat forward. 'Winston Smart turned up in Birmingham, months ago. He'd been living under false identities for a year. They arrested him trying to rob a post office.'

'Bully for them,' James stated, with a shrug of his shoulders. 'It's a matter of indifference to me. He can't do me any good, can't bring back my friend, can't bring back the girl.'

There was a moment's silence. He was conscious that Davis and Harland were studying him. He could see they weren't quite sure where they were with him, which turning to take now.

Harland said, 'Winston's singing like the proverbial bird – like he's auditioning for the dawn chorus.'

Davis, his expression darkening, added, 'You won't like the song he's singing. Not one bit.'

'It's about your friend Hickson,' Harland continued. 'We're hearing things about him you didn't tell us – we think out of a misplaced sense of loyalty.'

James glared at them. He didn't want to play games. Half an hour ago he'd been ready to leave this world, might yet make that journey before the sun set. What use was all this to him?

'You'd be better getting to the point,' he opined, his tone as cutting as a razor.

Davis leaned back, folded his arms. Harland cleared her throat.

'In a nutshell, then,' Davis said, 'Winston confirmed everything you told us about what happened in the yard and his dying man act to blackmail you into the Trinidad trip. He confirmed you knew the girl was carrying but didn't know about drugs in your suitcase. Over and above that—'

'Why would he do that now?' James cut in.

Harland explained. 'He thinks if he talks it'll help him get a reduced sentence.'

James looked from one detective to the other. 'So, one year on, you think I'm going to turn somersaults.' He sighed, long and deep. 'People died because of me.'

Into the silence that developed, Harland said softly, 'You knew Hickson was dealing, didn't you?'

James dropped his eyes to the floor. Hickson had been his friend once. He still had a vestige of honour, wasn't going to grass him up. Why ruin Hickson's life for his youthful mistakes? And there was Liz to consider. In spite of everything, her happiness meant something. He shook his head.

'What makes you think that?' he grunted.

'Because,' Davis said, 'Winston told us Hickson owed him £5,000 in drug money and couldn't pay. That was why he was beaten that night, how you became involved.'

An invisible hand clutched James's innards. Five thousand?

It wasn't credible. He knew Hickson had purchased drugs, but just for his circle of friends, for recreational use, nothing more. Not for one moment had he suspected he was involved to the tune of £5,000. He told himself it couldn't be. Winston must surely be lying for his own, nefarious ends.

'I don't believe it,' he said.

Davis gave him a long-suffering look. 'Hickson told Winston you and your friend beat him up, betrayed you in return for more time to pay up. Hardly the action of a good friend, or a person suffering amnesia, was it? Then cousin Bradley stepped in with his idea to use you in Trinidad.'

James felt his stomach muscles tighten. His throat constricted. All this was plausible, but that was all it was.

'Hickson wouldn't—' he stuttered.

'He took you for fools,' Harland said. 'Naïve fools.'

James screwed his eyes tight, put his head down as though by that action he could shut out the world. After a moment, he shook his head slowly.

'Hickson wouldn't.'

Davis said, 'There's more. How do you think they found the girl hiding in the flat?'

James opened his eyes, stared at the policeman. It was something he'd always wondered about.

'You went to Hickson, told him you had the girl and the drugs. In return for cancelling his debt, your friend told Winston, who passed that choice piece of information to cousin Bradley. You know how that ended, don't you?'

The policeman's words were like a stiletto in James's side. He slumped back in the chair, dug his fingers deep into the soft material of the arms as though he would never let go. It all made sense. It explained how the gangsters had picked them up so soon after the incident at the Blacksmith pub. Hickson was the only one who'd known about the girl in the flat. Only hours after he'd told him, the gangsters had turned up there. All this time he'd had suspicions but he'd shut them out, wouldn't let himself believe it was possible.

Harland slid the stiletto deeper. 'You were stitched, good and proper.'

The scales fell from his eyes. It was as though a light had suddenly shone in all those grey areas where the truth had been clear if only he'd let himself look. Everything bad that had happened reflected back to Hickson, his callous self-serving. What price loyalty to your friends? His own had been misplaced. Hickson must be laughing up his sleeve. He was prospering, had even married his girl. Another dark thought struck him. Perhaps part of Hickson's plan had been to get him out of the way so he could pursue Liz. Resentment stoked his anger. It took him all his time to compose himself.

'If you know all this, you must have arrested Hickson by now.'

Harland shook her head. 'Winston would testify. But we're not sure it would be enough. Hickson would have the best lawyers and they'd argue it was a crazy man's resentment of the system. How can you believe the word of a proven criminal, they'd say.'

'They'd say Winston Smart and I put our heads together, concocted it all.'

'You've got it in one,' Davis said.

'So you tell me all this knowing it won't go anywhere.' James let out a long sigh brimming with frustration. 'All you've really done is made me feel a thousand times worse.'

Both detectives were silent for a moment. Then Harland said, 'We had to tell you because now that you know you might remember something that can help us get him.'

James shrugged. 'I doubt there's anything.'

'Look son,' Davis said. 'We're thinking of using Winston to

provoke Hickson, to catch him off guard so that he slips up. But we need something that will really worry him – a dodgy friend, a place, an incident. We want you to think, son.'

James tugged at his beard. 'Clutching at straws, aren't we?'

'Just try,' Harland said.

Thoughts galloped through James's head like wild horses on the rampage. From the moment the sun had risen it had been an eventful day. His priest had spoken of redemption, acceptance of your own responsibility as the first step. Well, he'd accepted his guilt and his punishment, but this morning he'd wanted to end it all. Now, he had unfinished business. Exposing the truth in the interests of proper justice was a responsibility too, for Ted's family and his own, as much as for himself.

'OK,' he said. 'I'll try but don't bet on me coming up with anything.'

'Good lad!' Davis said, his expression brightening. 'The officer's outside. Go back to your cell and start thinking. We'll be in touch.'

James stood up and walked to the door. Harland followed, opened it for him.

'Remember you weren't the one who pulled the trigger, James,' she whispered. 'A little self-forgiveness wouldn't go amiss. I'm sure your friend Ted would tell you that if he could.'

Tears started to form at the corners of his eyes. He fought them back afraid the screw would see them.

'I wish he was here to tell me himself,' he mumbled and stepped out.

33

THE SCREW TOOK him back to his own block without a word, which suited James. Other inmates were up and about. One group was leaning casually on the gangway rails, like sailors at sea taking a break, staring out across a vast ocean of infinity. In reality, the limit of their vision was the opposite gangway, its cages exactly like their own. Some, James knew, accepted the confinement, saw it as an occupational hazard. Others, especially those facing long sentences, lost themselves in routine, never counted days or thought too far ahead because that way madness lay. Could he afford to let himself hope, he wondered?

'Home, sweet home,' the screw said as he unlocked the cell door and let James in. 'Free meals included. Lucky for some.'

James didn't bite. He'd learned not to retaliate. The more you did, the more they baited you. Why should he let them have their fun? The more unremarkable you were, the more invisible you became, and that was a good thing because there were screws in here whose minds were more twisted than those of many of the inmates.

When the door shut he tumbled on to the bed, lay on his back staring at the ceiling. In the privacy of his cell all those thoughts and emotions he'd been trying to control exploded like a myriad rockets. How could Hickson have been so evil and calculating and neither he, nor Ted, see it? His background had been different from theirs but they'd rubbed along well enough together. It pained him now to think how he had used them, how, beneath the show of *bonhomie*, he must have hated their guts. He felt his anger and resentment burgeoning and, for the first time for a long while, it was not directed inward but at his former friend, the architect of all his troubles. He remembered how his day had started. If he'd succeeded in killing himself, that would surely have suited Hickson, would have been another victory for him.

Wearied by a surfeit of emotion, he felt his eyelids droop. He fought the desire to sleep, tried to think back to the past, to his life with Hickson, searched for something that might help the detectives. But his roller-coaster of a day caught up with him. Sleep stole up on him and he started to drift off, Hickson's face haunting him.

He was back in the yard of the Blacksmith pub. Hickson was prone on the cobbles, Winston looming over him. He saw himself pick up the brick, bring it down on Winston's head, watched Winston shake himself and stagger away. Then Ted was standing over Hickson, holding a mobile phone, but a hand snaked out, grabbed the phone from him. A voice James knew didn't belong in that yard shouted out, something he couldn't understand. He woke with a start, disorientated. Then that same voice shouted again and he realized it was a prisoner in one of the cells venting his frustrations to the screws. He lay a while longer with his own sense of frustration, feeling as though he'd been on the verge of something important when his dream had been disturbed. He tried to grasp what it was but it lay wreathed in a fog, tantalizing him. Before he had time to give it more consideration a screw unlocked his door, announced that it was time to go to work.

Later that morning he was told to clean the floor in the kitchen. Working the mop across the floor, he let his mind wander over his past memories as Davis had asked him to do.

But he was getting nowhere. He began to think it was a waste of time, that there was nothing he knew that could incriminate Hickson. Did the detective really expect he'd know anything? He'd lived a normal student life, aware that Hickson bought a small quantity of drugs, blissfully unaware he was so involved in dealing.

He finished the floor, picked up the bucket ready to move on to his next job. His mind was preoccupied and, forgetting the floor was still wet, he slipped over and spilled dirty water where he'd just cleaned. Cursing his clumsiness, he fetched fresh water from the tap and started again. He'd barely begun when a memory sparked and he froze in mid-motion. The events in his dream replayed in his head but this time no voice interrupted the sequence and when it finished he knew what his subconscious had wanted him to remember. With any luck, it might help the detectives to convict Hickson.

34

DAVE HICKSON ADMIRED himself in the bedroom mirror. He liked the image: the pristine white shirt, the tie and the expensive pinstriped suit. As he removed an offending hair from his shoulder, he remembered how, on the council estate in Leeds that had spawned him, wearing a tie, never mind a suit, was hardly customary except perhaps for weddings and funerals. How his life had changed for the better! He considered he deserved his new-found status too. Sometimes it had been touch and go. He'd skirted the edge of the precipice enough times, especially with the Winston Smart business. But he was a winner, man enough to put himself on the line and, just at the end of the old time Hollywood movies, he'd finally won the money and the girl.

He heard a noise from downstairs, realized Liz was already in the kitchen and started to make his way down, reflecting how strange it felt to be a married man. Sometimes he had to pinch himself to believe it was all true. His persistence had won Liz and she'd come with a dowry in the form of this splendid house and a position with a well-respected law firm, courtesy of his father-in-law's influential contacts. His drug-dealing days were becoming a fading memory with each day of his new life.

"Morning, darling,' he said, as he entered the kitchen and eased himself into a chair.

She smiled at him. 'Where are you headed today?'

After a moment's hesitation, he said, 'Stockton Prison, of all places. Apparently a prospective client has asked for me by name, reckons he's heard good things about me so the boss wants me to interview him.'

He watched her carefully, just for a second thought he saw a flicker of sadness pass across her face and knew the reason.

'You're thinking of James,' he said, his tone soft, concerned. 'Sorry – when I mentioned prison, especially one on Teesside ...'

She raised her eyes to meet his, shook her head. 'Not your fault. It's just sometimes I can hardly believe what happened, how James and Ted could risk everything the way they did.' She drew in a breath, then continued, 'Sometimes I think I – we – should visit James, don't you, Dave?'

He glanced at her meaningfully, stretched for the teapot and poured himself a cup. 'We've been over this. James made his bed and he's part of the past now. Besides, we've our good name to consider.'

He watched her face, hoping he hadn't spoken too bluntly. Liz had a mind of her own and, if he came over too dictatorial, she might well rebel to prove a point. Logic was his best weapon where she was concerned and he knew her weak points.

'In the circles we move in, consorting with criminals might come back to haunt us,' he continued. 'Careers can depend on such matters. There must be no doubt about my – our – probity. You see that, don't you, dear?'

He saw he'd hit a nerve. Liz was ambitious for both of them. Anything standing in the way of their careers or status would give her pause for thought.

'It's hard to think of James as a criminal. He denied anything to do with drug dealing, didn't he?'

'Wouldn't you?'

She shrugged. 'I suppose so.'

He stood up, put an arm around her shoulder. 'Time heals, dear. Let go of the past. You and I have a great future together.'

He was glad to see her smile. She followed him to the door, waved to him when he drove off in the Jaguar and he blew her a kiss. When he reached the motorway he relaxed into the drive. Teesside was an hour away from the small hamlet in the Yorkshire dales where he was living. If that little outburst at breakfast was anything to go by, he was glad Liz hadn't offered to come with him to visit their old stamping grounds for old times' sake. What was the saying? The moving finger writes and then moves on. Well, that was his philosophy. In this life you didn't waste time turning back pages. The past was another land where dreamers wasted time while everybody rushed past them and trod on their dreams. His mind turned to the prisoner he was going to visit. His name was George Silva and he'd asked specifically for him. Hickson smiled to himself. He'd hardly started and he was gaining a reputation. Way to go, as the Americans would say.

He arrived at the prison on time. After he'd gone through security an officer escorted him, unlocking door after door in a labyrinth of corridors until eventually they entered an interview room set aside for legal visits. He was told he'd have to wait there, that another officer based on Silva's wing would bring the prisoner to see him. The officer said he'd remain with him in the room, make sure it happened.

The room was small and bare. Hickson felt offended that persons of his status should have to conduct business in surroundings hardly more salubrious than those the prisoners would be accustomed to. The furniture consisted of two hard chairs and a desk adorned with coffee stains. He sat at the desk and waited.

Five minutes passed. He didn't like to be kept waiting and was growing impatient. The officer watched him fiddling with the clasp of his briefcase with what looked like a twinkle of amusement in his eyes. Hickson didn't like that, nor the fellow's supercilious expression. Why did he merit his attentions anyway, when there were a thousand inmates in this jail to supervise. One day one of them, in the wrong mood, would probably rearrange the fellow's face for him if he looked at him like that. He supposed one blessing was that the fellow hadn't attempted conversation.

That small mercy didn't last, however. 'Time is money, eh, sir?'

Hickson thought he could detect more than a touch of envy in the officer's tone. He stopped fiddling with the clasp, glared across the room and decided to feed his envy.

Affecting an air of ennui, he commented. 'You could say this place is like one big factory for me, with you fellows employed to look after my assets. So, in a way, your time is my money, isn't it?'

There wasn't a flicker on the officer's face. He seemed blissfully unaware he'd just been on the receiving end of a put-down.

Grinning, he said, 'You must make a lot of lolly at Her Majesty's pleasure, sir?'

Hickson raised a quizzical eyebrow in his direction. Couldn't this fellow take a hint? Was he as thick as those stupid enough to be caught and incarcerated here under the charge of people like him? Or was he just persisting in his insolence out of jealousy of Hickson's position? For sure, he wouldn't be able to afford a suit like the one Hickson was wearing.

'Don't you worry,' Hickson came back at him. 'I intend to make a lot more lolly.'

The officer said nothing, just grinned and a long silence

developed. Hickson decided he might as well kill a little time by picking the fellow's brain, limited though it surely was. He grasped the papers he'd placed on the desk, wafted them in the air.

'This fellow, Silva. Know him, do you?'

A gleam came into the officer's eye. 'Goes to the chapel, he does. One of the converted. One of your God squad.'

Hickson puffed out his cheeks. 'With a record like his, it'll take more than religious mania to help him when he's in front of a jury. The scales won't drop from their eyes.'

'C of E myself, sir. Never did me any harm. Helps to believe in something in this madhouse.'

As he finished speaking the door opened and another officer stepped into the room. The prisoner was behind him in the corridor but mostly hidden by the officer's bulk.

'Silva for you, sir,' the officer announced with military curtness and stood aside to let the man enter.

Hickson's first impression of his client was of a mop of black hair sprouting in all directions. As Silva advanced into the room, he kept his head down. That, combined with the cascading hair, made it difficult to see his face properly. He came so far, then seemed to hesitate.

'Come on, man, take a seat,' Hickson said, not wanting to waste any more time.

The prisoner shuffled forward again as though his feet were restricted by chains. There was an aura of servility about him not just confined to his movement. Hickson's immediate thought was that here was a man whom prison had broken. Against that, he knew that many prisoners were con merchants. What you saw was often far away from what you got, though what this fellow would have to gain from deceiving him he couldn't imagine. Perhaps he thought he could win sympathy, use it to his advantage – pigs might fly.

He nodded to each officer in turn. 'That'll be all.'

The officers exchanged knowing glances and started for the door. Before he left the room, the one who had escorted the prisoner from the wing turned to address him.

'We'll just be outside.' He pointed to a green buzzer on the wall next to the door. 'Press that if you need us.'

Hickson exaggerated his smile, its subtext as clear as he intended it to be. Why would he need them? He was perfectly capable of dealing with this abject creature.

'I won't need nursemaids,' he grunted.

Once they were in the corridor the two prison officers leaned against a whitewashed wall. A look which conveyed a mutual opinion passed between them.

The one who'd had to wait with Hickson raised his eyebrows disdainfully.

'Snotty-nosed, condescending bastard, that one,' he muttered.

'I take it you mean the prisoner,' Silva's escorting officer responded with a sly grin and a twinkle in his eye.

His colleague appeared perplexed for a moment. Then, understanding the irony, he shook his head and laughed.

'The prisoner probably has more manners. Give me a straight-up villain every time in preference to a jumped-up solicitor. Like leeches they are, except you can burn leeches off.'

The escorting officer smiled enigmatically as though he possessed secret knowledge he wasn't prepared to share.

'I just started here last week, moved up from the south,' he said, 'but one thing I do know – it's a universal truth.'

'Go on then, Socrates.'

The reply came with a conspiratorial wink. 'What goes around comes around. They all know it in here, deep down in their twisted souls. Karma, mate. You can't beat it.'

'Yeah! Yeah! Heard it before. It doesn't apply to his type. It's money that comes back to the likes of him.'

The escorting officer tapped his nose. 'Just you wait and see. There's forces at work. Take my word.'

35

HICKSON WAS LOSING patience. His eyes flicked between the fly crawling on the desk and the papers in his hand, then returned to the convict. The fellow had not raised his head since he'd entered the room and had answered his preliminary questions with guttural monosyllabics. Hell's teeth, what had he got here? Was this Silva mentally unstable, or just giving a passable imitation? The fly did a little leap and landed near his hand, adding to his irritation. Who knew what diseases the dirty little germ-carrier could spread in a place like this? He bunched his fist, brought it down with a loud thump, squashing the insect. That'll wake the fellow up, he thought. But the prisoner hadn't even flinched.

He started to feel uncomfortable. The convict's impassivity was surely unnatural. What on earth was going on in his mind?

'For God's sake lift your head, man,' he commanded. 'I'll have to see your face if we're going to talk.'

At last the prisoner raised his head, looked straight at him. Hickson frowned; he was sure he knew that face from somewhere. The cogs in his memory turned, came to a rude halt. As though a snake was about to strike out at him, he recoiled. Just for a second he thought he must be mistaken. But then, beyond doubt, he knew. The hair might be longer, the face much thinner and haggard, but this Silva was Winston Smart in the flesh. Fear engulfed him then, like a shark's jaws with teeth poised to tear him apart. He leapt to his feet, staggered backwards, stared at the buzzer near the door. It seemed an ocean away.

'Livin' ghosts. They the worst kind, man.' Winston said.

The familiar voice was a superfluous confirmation that the prisoner was his former tormentor. Hickson's thoughts ran amok now. Was this a set-up? Had the gangster violent intentions towards him? Did he have a hidden weapon?

Once again he stared at the alarm, his only lifeline. Winston hadn't made any kind of move, didn't look as though he was in any kind of hurry, looked too confident in fact. He decided he had to take a chance, risk going for it. Eyes moving incessantly, he edged round the desk.

Winston still didn't move, just sat there calmly. There was a look in his eyes as though he was in complete control of the situation.

'I ain't looking to kill you or nothing,' he said, levelly. 'You press that buzzer, you harm yourself. Your whole life turn upside down. You be ruined, man.'

Hickson heard but kept moving. What did Winston mean, he'd be ruined, and why was he so cool? He took another step which brought him level with the gangster's chair. Winston didn't even turn his head. He thought about making a rush for the buzzer; as soon as he pressed it officers would come running. Yet he hesitated, still confused because Winston was just sitting there like a meditating Buddhist seeking his nirvana. What could he possibly have on him that gave him such confidence?

Winston turned his head to face him now, his eyebrows down. 'Your friend James Harper and me – we know things. You need to listen.'

That took Hickson by surprise. Was it possible that the gangster and his old flatmate had met in prison? If that was so,

Winston could have enlightened James, who would be vengeful. Was he behind this, Winston just his messenger boy?

'I don't think James Harper would pass the time of day with your kind,' he stated, searching the gangster's face for a reaction.

Winston studied his fingernails with an air of insouciance.

'Times change. We reconciled. Prison done that.' Winston narrowed his eyes.

'James didn't tell anybody who you really are?'

'He knows what happen to grasses in prison.'

Hickson tilted his head to one side. His brow wrinkled.

'James Harper attacked you with a brick, did you physical damage and now you're big buddies. You expect me to believe that?'

Winston wafted a hand in the air. 'That gone now. He recognizes me in here so I approach him, tell him how you stitch him – two times. He get madder and madder. He hit the wall so hard he bust his hand. He want to know why you did it.'

Hickson was quiet as he digested this. If it was true, it was worrying. But what could James do to him at the end of the day, even with Winston to back up his story? Who would believe the word of two criminals? Their version would be seen as a fiction. What solid proof could they produce? He felt his confidence revive a little.

'So the two of you intend to get together and talk to the police. Am I right?'

'Loud man! Loud!' Winston leaned towards Hickson, his eyes much more animated now. 'Unless you give us – consideration.'

Hickson snorted. Blackmail didn't sound like James's style. Of course, there was always the possibility that Winston was acting on his own, his collusion with James made up.

'And what form would this consideration take?'

More like the man Hickson remembered from the past, Winston stared at him hard like an animal at its prey.

'Ten thousand is what we want from you, man.'

Into the silence, from beyond the barred window a crow cawed and another answered it. It sounded like scornful laughter. Hickson was turning it over. End of the day, ten thousand wasn't much but why should he pay when he didn't think anybody would believe them?

'James Harper wouldn't settle for money. He'd want blood. I think you're doing this alone. Even if you're not, you have no definite proof, either of you.'

Winston smiled enigmatically. 'Think of your reputation, man. What they say? Mud sticks?'

Hickson glowered. Winston had a point there. But he didn't intend to pay up without a fight. The gangster was probably bluffing about James's involvement to add more force to his threat. If he played it cool, let him think he wasn't bothered, he might just give it up as a bad job.

'I've lived through worse things. I'd survive. People might even feel sorry for me, the victim of a gangster so spiteful he makes unjust accusations.' He stroked his chin. 'You'd have to have more or you're wasting your time.'

They locked eyes in a contest of wills. Hickson saw something stirring in his opponent's which disturbed him. He'd forgotten the violence in the man for a moment. Fearing he was about to turn nasty, he glanced at the buzzer, readied himself to make a rush for it if he had to.

But the gangster didn't move, 'I got more than stories,' he snapped. 'Your friend give it to me.'

'I don't think so. I've always been careful, tidied up after me.'

'Careless with your phone though,' Winston said, with a triumphant grin. 'Your friend hides your phone and forgets about it. He don't realize what the police can do with it, how they can make it talk back, tell them things – like maybe all the drug dealers you do business with.'

Hickson felt the blood drain from his face. This was bad. If that phone was resurrected, it would harm him. He swallowed hard.

'You know where it is, I presume?'

'A man pick it up for me any time I say.'

'And James? He's willing to return it to me?'

Winston smiled, white teeth gleaming. 'He got time to do and money help in prison – like anywhere.'

Hickson swallowed hard. No doubt about it, if the phone fell into the hands of the police it could be used against him. It would be hard evidence that he was in contact with known drug dealers. Under pressure, some of those dealers would testify against their own granny. He couldn't see a way out other than to get that phone back. Staked against the threat of ruin, ten thousand was paltry. And once he had the phone, they wouldn't be able to hurt him any more, or come back to bleed him dry.

'I'll pay the ten thousand for the phone,' he said.

Silva nodded. 'Thought so.'

'How?'

'I got people out there. You be hearing when and where. Just make sure you deliver in person.'

An uneasy silence descended. Winston made the first move, rising from his chair.

'Keep to it, man,' he said. 'You don't – I got a long reach.'

The gangster moved to the door, turned to face Hickson. Looking into Winston's face, its brute ugliness, Hickson remembered what the officer had told him about his religious conversion. In his resentment, he couldn't resist a barb.

'Thought you'd got religion,' he sneered. 'Didn't know the deal offered special dispensation to blackmailers.'

Winston grinned. 'Silva got religion. Winston still a bad ass.'

'So Winston will keep the money, won't give James Harper a share?'

'He'll get it,' Winston said. 'Us bad asses got a code in prison. A deal is a deal.' He started for the door. 'Man like you wouldn't understand.'

He rapped on the door. One of the officers opened it and he stepped out without a backward glance.

The same officer put his head round the door a moment later. 'You all right, sir. You look like you've seen a ghost.'

Pulling at his collar, Hickson stammered. 'It's the … lack of air in here.'

'My colleague will take you out soon, sir,' the officer told him and closed the door.

Hickson slumped down in the chair, breathed a loud sigh and cursed the hand fate had played him. One little thing he'd forgotten about had returned to plague him, had the potential to ruin him. Fortunately, he had the money to stop that happening, to buy back his life, and the sooner he had the phone in his possession the better he'd feel.

As he drove away from the prison he was tempted to call the governor, tell him he had a prisoner, Silva, residing there under a false identity. But he knew that could have repercussions for himself. Perhaps later, when he had the phone back, he'd do it, give himself a little satisfaction.

36

A WEEK AFTER his ill-fated visit to Stockton Prison, Hickson was in his office when the phone call he'd been expecting came through. A gruff voice gave him the meeting place and told him the exchange would be made the next day. If he wasn't there with the cash, he'd have to suffer the consequences. He was glad things were moving because the waiting and wondering was getting to him. Garnering the £10,000 had been easy enough. Liz, fortunately, took no interest in their financial affairs, probably wouldn't even notice it was missing. He figured she was so used to having plenty, she didn't watch over their wealth with the same solicitude as he did himself.

The next day he drove up to Teesside, parked his Jaguar near the gates of Albert Park, not that far from his old university. Two youths, about the age to be students, strolled out of the park gates, passed by the car. They had a carefree air about them as they laughed and joked and it struck him that he was looking at a mirror image of himself as he had been not that long ago. They also reminded him how far he'd risen in a short time and how he'd hate to fall back down now.

It had been threatening to rain. Now the threat became manifest as a gentle pitter-patter on the car roof which grew until it became a relentless drumming. Hickson glanced once again at the briefcase on the passenger seat, consoled himself with the thought that what he had to gain by handing over its contents was cheap at the price.

Through the slanting rain he peered out at the café across the road. He'd never been inside but remembered it had a place in local lore. The old-time soccer stars had gathered there after training. He wondered how many transfer deals had been first mooted inside, how many illicit 'bungs' had been handed over in brown paper bags. Well, it was his turn today to continue the tradition, but with much more at stake.

The clock on the dashboard moved to 3 p.m., time for him to move. He pulled his raincoat over his shoulders, picked up the briefcase. Gripping it tight, he climbed out of the car and made a run for it, accelerating between a gap in the traffic.

Inside the café, the décor was basic, functional rather than an attempt at anything ornate. An aroma that Hickson identified as fried onions mingling with coffee beans drifted into his nostrils and he worried that the odour would linger on his suit, cause a caustic comment from Liz when he got home. Chiding himself for that foolish thought when he had much more serious matters to contend with, he shook the rain out of his hair, approached the counter and ordered a coffee. A dark-haired girl with gypsy eyes served him. She looked him up and down as though she thought, dressed the way he was, he'd wandered in by mistake, or was a health and hygiene inspector on a mission.

The café was half-full, mainly of older women returning from shopping expeditions stopping off for late afternoon gossip, too engrossed to take too much notice of him. He carried his coffee to a window table, placed his briefcase on the seat so that his body sheltered it in case a sneak thief decided to chance his arm.

He wiped his neck where the rain had crept under his collar, supped his coffee while he waited. Then, a few minutes after his own entrance, a smart middle-aged man came in. The newcomer took a moment to shake his umbrella and fold it before marching to the counter. Hickson's first impression was that he didn't look anything like Winston's type in manner or dress, so he couldn't be his contact. He was expecting someone rough-looking. It was a surprise to him when the man approached his table.

'Raining on our parade, isn't it, Mr Hickson?'

Hickson stared at him, then nodded. The man squeezed into the seat opposite, put his coffee down. Everything about him went against expectation. This was no flamboyantly attired West Indian with a gold necklace – Winston's kind. This was a middle-aged man dressed in a blazer, his features refined, more like a priest's than a gangster's. He looked as though he'd be more at home in a Conservative club. Leaning forward, he glanced at the briefcase, a sparkle in his eye.

'You have something for me, I believe.'

'First I need to see what you've got for me.'

The man gave a wry smile, opened his jacket just long enough for Hickson to see he was wearing a shoulder holster with a gun in it.

'Just insurance,' he said, then reached inside his pocket, brought out a mobile phone and laid it on the table. Hickson was almost certain he recognized it as his.

'Take a closer look,' the man said, 'If you need to make sure.'

Hickson hesitated. He couldn't help feeling that something wasn't right. The fellow just didn't look the type to be one of Winston's social circle and his accent had been refined, not unlike that of the people in his own profession.

Seeming to sense his doubts, the man spoke up. 'Don't let appearances fool you. I'm just out of prison myself. Went down for armed robbery. You make pals for life in there. Winston and James were big buddies of mine, hence this little favour.'

Hickson figured he had to chance it. He slid his hand towards the phone, picked it up. Examining it closely, he knew for sure it was his. He glanced around the café. Nobody was showing any interest. So far, so good. As soon as he'd handed the money over, he'd be out of there, life back on track.

'The phone's mine all right.'

The man stared at Hickson, eyebrows arching. 'So there is only the matter of the phone bill now.'

Hickson placed the mobile in his pocket, put the briefcase on the table. The man pulled it on to his lap, checked the contents, smiled at him.

'Winston told me to tell you he won't bother you again.'

With the phone back in his possession, Hickson felt more confident. 'If he does, I've enough money to buy protection, to have him killed if necessary.'

The man's face showed no reaction. He rose, picked up the briefcase and his umbrella.

'Yes, sir,' he said with mock servility then walked away from the table.

Hickson watched him walk past the window. The steam on the glass was like a veil between them, giving him a ghostly appearance, as though he was already part of the past. Hickson drained his cup, pleased it was over and done with.

It was still raining when he stepped outside. He was so relieved, he couldn't have cared less. With his coat on his arm, he ran across the road like a boy released early from school.

He was reaching for the car door, vowing it would be a long time before he returned to Middlesbrough and not caring if it was never. Suddenly, a hand clutched his shoulder and he felt fingers digging into his flesh like talons. His body flinched in natural reaction and his adrenaline surged. Was he about to be mugged?

He whirled around, lips drawing back, showing his teeth like a feral creature ready to defend itself. The face staring into his was familiar, caused him to rein in. It took him a moment to recognize Detective Inspector Davis and, a few steps behind him, the young woman with her hair flattened by the rain. He fought down his panic. What were these two doing here? Had they been watching him in the café? Those bony fingers hadn't relented. Surely he wasn't going to be arrested.

'I like the rain, son,' Davis said. 'Afterwards everything's so clean and pure, isn't it?'

Hickson blinked the rain out of his eyes, tried to calm himself and mumbled, 'Is it?'

The woman stepped up. 'All that money,' she said, shaking her head. 'And you didn't even leave a tip.'

'The more they have …' Davis added with a supercilious grin.

Hickson's panic shot up the scale. These two knew what had happened in the café. How much else did they know?'

Davis released his grip, reached inside Hickson's pocket, extracted the phone.

'Can't let the rain damage it, can we?' he said, sliding it into his pocket with a satisfied grin. 'Not after all the trouble you've gone to. Not after what it cost you.'

Hickson's mouth went dry. He dredged for words, came up empty. They must know everything. He was fenced in, no gaps to bolt for.

'You blabbed in the prison and you were taped,' Davis continued. 'Now you've blabbed in the café to our colleague who was wired. With Winston ready to testify, and what we expect to get from the mobile, you're toast, son.'

Hickson dropped his head. Like the rain swirling down the drain at his feet, all his dreams were vanishing into a black hole. For once, he couldn't think of anything to say. But Davis could and said it, with obvious relish.

'Arrest this nasty piece of work, Diane.'

The detective constable looked him in the eye, gave him the spiel. The words of his formal arrest hit him like a physical blow. When she'd finished and they led him away the rain pelted against his face and body like justice from the heavens held back far too long and trying to make amends for its tardiness.

'Satisfied now, sir, are we?' Harland asked her boss. They were in Davis's office. Davis was standing by the radiator trying to dry his socks. He glanced at her quizzically.

She continued, 'You were never happy with the way that case ended. You always thought James Harper wasn't as involved as he appeared to be.' She ran a comb through her wet hair. 'Well, you were right and the truth is out.'

Davis smiled. 'Would that the truth was always out. I wonder how many times we get all the guilty parties.'

Harland removed her coat, sat down and wiped her face with a paper tissue. 'If Winston Smart hadn't agreed to help snare Hickson – why did he co-operate so readily, sir?'

'I told him it might get his sentence reduced.' Davis looked down at his bare feet. 'Also I committed the sin of omission, like that boyfriend of yours, the one who neglected to tell you he was engaged.'

She gave him a hard stare that told him not to go any further down that route, then said, 'So what didn't we tell Winston Smart – to outsmart him?'

Davis screwed up his nose. 'Your patter smells worse than my socks.'

'Come on, sir. Tell!'

Davis sighed. 'He was under the impression that Hickson informed us Bradley and gang were in the students' flat, maintained he did it hoping he would be there too. Got really worked up about it. I didn't deny it and he wanted to pay Hickson back.'

She shook her head. 'Useful, that sin of omission. Maybe I'll try it on you sometime.'

Davis laughed. 'It's helped James Harper anyway.'

'That young man has a lot to thank you for, sir. He'll get an earlier release now there's mitigating factors.'

'He was very foolish and has paid the price. Let's hope he can pick up the pieces and put himself together again.'

'And Hickson, sir?'

Davis snorted. 'Different kettle of fish. A real piece of work that one. Deserves all he gets.'

37

THE PRISON PADRE droned on. Winston wasn't listening to a word. The tea and cakes the holy man habitually provided, the real reason for enduring his homilies, had already been consumed. Winston was a regular attender at these weekly gatherings. Today, though, he intended to satisfy more than his appetite for sweet things and a desire for a change from looking at the walls of his cell.

Bolt, one of the ten prisoners gathered in the small room that served as chapel, nudged his elbow. It was rumoured that back in Jamaica the Yardie had killed thirteen men in the gang wars. Unlucky for some, Winston thought, and maximum respect to the man.

'You gonna do it, right?' Bolt's soft, melodic voice contradicted his reputation.

Winston didn't turn his head. 'Yeah, man. No worries.'

'I hear they moves him soon. You never get another chance, maybe.'

Back in the days, when they were fledglings in Jamaica, Bolt had known cousin Bradley, spoke highly of him too. Including Bolt, there were seven Yardies on Winston's wing. When he'd told them how Bradley had died, how a little weasel had set him up, to a man they'd said the weasel had to die. Ratting on the weasel wasn't enough. Yardie respect needed blood for blood, they'd told him, and it was his responsibility to take care of business. Bradley was his kin, would expect it of him. Their good opinion mattered to Winston and he didn't want to lose face, particularly in the dog-eat-dog world of prison. Given the bad news he'd received a week ago, he figured he had nothing to lose anyway.

'Pass the shiv, man,' he said.

Bolt felt inside his shirt, pulled out the makeshift knife. Constructed of a piece of fined-down metal pilfered from the workshops and bound to a toothbrush handle with twine, it wasn't much to look at but would serve. Winston took it from him and hid it inside his own shirt.

'How'd you get it in here?' Winston whispered.

Bolt grinned. 'That screw who brought us. I got pictures of him with one of my bitches.' Bolt patted his trouser pocket. 'Now I got him in here like he was a little mouse.'

Winston shifted his eye to the table in front of them. It was draped in a white cloth and a small silver cross sat in the middle in a failed attempt to lend sanctity to the bleak room. Today, if all went well, it would be used for a much more profane purpose. Winston recalled a teacher rattling on about a Trojan horse. Well, he'd kick some life back into that old story today. He'd be the talk of the prison, might even make the papers – maximum respect.

He brought his attention back to the padre who was winding down, finishing off one of his stories which was full of platitudes he'd heard a thousand times before and, except for that thing about an eye for an eye, meant nothing in his world.

'Now that we have heard the Lord's word,' the padre was saying, his voice rising, 'let us mingle in good fellowship. Discuss amongst yourselves what you have heard until it is time to return to your wing, replenished in spirit, I hope. Should any of you wish to address me further on matters arising today, feel free to come forth.'

'Praise the Lord,' one of the men shouted, not out of rapture but from relief. His fellow inmates sniggered.

As he always did at the end of one of his sessions, the padre retired to a desk in a corner of the room. He sat down, pushed grey straggles of hair out of his eyes, picked up a book and lost himself in his reading.

'You ready?' Bolt asked.

'Let's do it,' Winston replied.

Bolt nudged the man on his other side. They both got to their feet, strolled lazily towards the desk. Bolt said something to the priest who looked up. The other prisoner spoke then and soon the padre was engaged in an earnest discussion. Winston waited until the padre's view was obscured by their bulk, then made his move. On tiptoe, he stole across the room, crouched down, lifted the white cloth and crawled under the table.

Balanced on his haunches, he felt like a kid playing a game of hide-and-seek. Minutes dragged by. He could hear conversations going on around him but knew nobody would dare give him away. Fortunately, the padre, in that nice little world of his own somewhere between this world and the next, would never suspect that one of the flock he was nurturing would betray his trust. It was that weakness in him that made him less vigilant than he should have been. Bolt, a master of manipulation, had observed it and seized on it when he'd helped Winston make his plan.

He tried lying flat on his belly and found that in that position there was just enough gap between the cloth and floor for him to be able to see most of the room, including the door. He focused on the door. Everything depended on timing: that nothing different happened today from what happened on other days, so it was a relief when, moments later, the door opened and the screw stepped inside right on time.

'The good shepherd's here for you, boys,' he shouted. 'But he won't need his crook, will he? Not with you lot in the pen.'

The prisoners groaned at his lack of imagination; they'd heard his poor joke before. Under the table, Winston tensed. Every plan needed luck. This was a crucial moment. He watched the men rise and make for the door where they formed a queue. The screw patted them down and let them out one by one, counting heads. Bolt positioned himself at the back of the queue, the last man. When it was his turn, the screw frowned. Bolt spoke to him. Winston held his breath. He was aware that Bolt was explaining they were a man down because one of them had been removed for a legal visit. The screw nodded and let Bolt out without searching him. Winston breathed again. So far, so good.

'Numbers correct, sir,' the screw shouted to the padre who was still at his desk. 'No stray sheep.'

A man of little imagination, the screw always used those words at the end of the session. Bolt had noted the habit, and the imprecision that meant they could be taken either as statements of facts or questions. Careless of practicalities, the padre never counted heads anyway. Unless the padre suddenly became security conscious, Winston figured the plan would work out.

'Thank you, officer,' the padre's voice boomed. 'The Lord numbers all his sheep and the shepherd too.'

Winston saw the screw grin, watched him step out and shut the door behind him. He gave a relieved sigh. It wouldn't be too long before the screws on the wing noticed he was missing. He just hoped the vulnerable prisoners would arrive in the chapel on time. After it was done, he'd be the man, no doubt about it. Long after he was gone, they'd talk about him.

He only had to wait a few minutes before the door opened again and a different screw entered. The padre wasn't in

Winston's line of vision. He figured he was probably at his desk.

'Ready to roll, sir,' the screw shouted.

'Send them in, please,' the padre's voice answered.

Flat on his belly, dust irritating his nostrils so he had to resist the urge to sneeze, Winston watched the newcomers troop in. He started to worry that perhaps his man wouldn't turn out today, might be ill or decide he'd had enough of the padre's Bible thumping, that the trade-off for tea and cakes wasn't worth the boredom. At first he couldn't see him and he started to panic. Then he spotted red hair and zeroed in. The face beneath the hair was gaunt, prison-pallid, and the scruffy, prison issue blue-striped shirt was far removed from the man's former sartorial elegance. But it was definitely his man. He watched him take a seat sit in the front row, then he drew further back under the table and eased up on to his haunches.

'That's your lot,' he heard the screw shout. 'The crème de la crème.'

The door banged as the screw shut it behind him. Winston felt inside his shirt for the shiv. He was sweating now, had to wipe his hands. The defining moment in the story of his life had arrived. After it was done, there'd be no escape. Of course, that was of little concern to him now. Do this right and he'd be going out as a top man, a name. He gripped the knife harder, clutched the white tablecloth, filled his cheeks with air and burst forth.

The congregated prisoners froze in their seats, mouths agape, as though the devil had somehow conjured himself in human form before their eyes. His face contorted, Winston didn't give them time to digest what was happening. All his concentration was on Dave Hickson. As he reached him, his arm shot out. The blade pressed into his neck far enough for a trickle of blood to flow. Hickson's neck snapped back. His eyes bulged with terror but he couldn't move a muscle because of the blade. Winston forced himself to hold back, wanting to see his fear, enjoying the power, the control over life and death. He wanted to relish his moment.

'You always take me for a fool, mister lawyer man!' he yelled.

Hickson's eyes flickered rapidly from side to side, appealing for help. But the other men had already moved away, were watching with morbid fascination.

'They too scared,' Winston snarled. 'They not normals, like you they *ab*-normals.'

From somewhere behind, the padre's tremulous voice pleaded, 'Leave him be.'

Winston twisted his head. The padre was seated at his desk. Winston didn't consider him a threat. He was soft: all words, no action.

'This man going to Hell,' Winston said.

'No!' Hickson squealed.

The shiv pressed further into his flesh. 'You tell police my cousin is in that flat,' Winston shouted. 'Make a fool of me.'

'Not me!' Hickson's voice emerged as a strangulated groan.

Winston smiled. 'Never did like you, man.'

In one smooth movement, he drew the blade across Hickson's throat. A jet of blood spurted and covered Winston's shirt with a red stain. The prisoners let out a collective groan of horror, then the room became silent except for the padre whimpering like a puppy. As his mouth dropped open and his eyes turned to glass, Hickson's face lost all expression. Finally, when the last of his life had ebbed away, his head lolled to one side and his body slumped in the chair. Winston watched in fascination. He wanted to see this man die close up, wanted to know what happened as your life was stolen from you. What could lie behind that blank stare? He guessed he'd find out for himself soon enough, but his money was on nothing at all, just oblivion.

The prisoners edged further away afraid that in his madness, he might turn on them. Still behind his desk, the padre was straight and rigid like a soldier paying last respects to a dead comrade. His wide-eyed expression conveyed that he was in shock, unable to move. Winston kept hold of the knife. As though he was on a country stroll, looking neither to left or right, he strode down the aisle and pressed the alarm. Folding his arms, he leaned against the wall as though he was waiting for a bus and was bored. He was thinking: Hickson was lucky in a way. His had been a quick death. His own was going to take a year and the cancer wasn't going to be as kind as the blade. The only saving grace was that he'd die respected.

38

EIGHT MONTHS AFTER Hickson's arrest, James Harper stood nervously at the prison door. When it swung open the three other prisoners due for release pushed through like eager shoppers at a sale. He held back, a little afraid. He was grateful that the truth had come to light. When the pressure he'd been under from the gangsters was understood, his case had been reviewed, his sentence shortened. Now, one step away from his freedom, he felt like an immigrant about to step off the boat into an alien land. His experiences, his life in prison, had changed him. How could it not have done? Could he cope with the changes, the different life he'd be living outside, the shame riding on his back?

The officer touched his arm. 'On you go, son, embrace the big, wide world and don't come back to Hell again.'

He took a deep breath, stepped outside. Instantly, he felt the welcoming warmth of the sun on his prison-pallid skin and a light wind ruffling his hair as gently as a woman's fingers. He savoured the experience as he watched the other prisoners embrace loved ones who were waiting for them with open arms. Suddenly he felt a different embrace, cold hands touching him all over as a feeling of loneliness overcame him. Nobody was here to meet him, but that was his own doing; he'd told his parents not to come, that he'd let them know when he was ready to see them. One day, God willing, he might feel worthy to be their son again.

He adjusted the brown-paper parcel which he held under his arm and which contained a change of clothes. With only a vague notion of where he was heading, content to be just moving away from everything behind him, he started walking.

Soulless, industrial warehouses surrounded the prison but to James, after his confinement, they had a certain beauty. In prison he'd had a recurring dream where he'd launch himself from a high mountain, expect to fall, only to discover he could fly over the countryside like an eagle. It had been exhilarating and he felt something of that same feeling now. After living in a cramped cell, the road ahead seemed to go on for ever with the promise of vistas of freedom waiting just for him. But soon he found himself in Stockton and things changed. The roar of car engines, people bustling around him, was too much, an assault on his senses after the prison quietness. He needed respite, so he allowed his long-held dream of a pint of beer to get the better of him and entered the nearest pub.

Using a little of the paltry amount of money he had been given on release, he bought a pint, carried it to a quiet corner. As he crossed the floor, people glanced up at him and he felt self-conscious, wondered whether he was being hypersensitive in thinking they could sense the stamp of prison on him.

Once he was seated he kept his head down, supped his beer, savouring the taste. When he did glance up, he noticed a female figure watching him from across the room. To his surprise she started forward in his direction. Like the chords of a sad song, the way she moved evoked a past memory he couldn't quite capture. He focused harder on her face. What was it about her? Then, suddenly, he knew. The hair was much shorter and she'd put on a little weight, but without doubt it was Liz striding out of the past towards him.

She halted a yard from him, uncertain. He tried to find words, failed. She was the last person he wanted to see. As he met her gaze, old emotions and old memories intermingled and he fought them down.

'Mrs Hickson, I presume,' he said at last, raising his glass in salute.

Hurt leapt into her eyes. 'Can I sit, please?' she asked in a small voice.

He inclined his head at the vacant chair. 'Feel free. This isn't a prison.'

He hadn't intended the irony and realized how casually he'd spoken the words, how easily they'd tripped off his tongue. In his old life, he'd taken freedom and everything else for granted. Looking as wary as a child who has done mischief and awaits chastisement, Liz slid into the chair.

'I'm so sorry, James,' she said. Her voice caught and she cleared her throat. 'I've followed you all the way from the prison to tell you that.'

His laugh was mirthless. 'It's your cousin Ted you should be sorry for. I haven't much in the way of prospects right now, but at least I have my life.'

Her eyes filled up. Taking a handkerchief from her pocket, she dabbed at them.

'I've been a fool,' she said. 'I had no idea what kind of man Hickson was. I knew he was a risk-taker and that attracted me – but the extent—'

'You never visited me, Liz. Was that because he stopped you? Or by choice?'

Her cheeks flushed. She put her head down. James didn't say anything and it was a few moments before she was able to look into his face.

'He discouraged me,' she said. 'But I can't make him my excuse. I could have come alone – should have.'

James nodded. He was thinking at least she was being truthful and truth hadn't been in ready supply in his life.

'And what is it you want from me, Liz, today of all days?'

She placed a hand on the table between them. He had the impression she wanted him to reach out and take it but he made no move.

In a small voice, she said, 'What I want most is for you to forgive me, James.'

'There's nothing to forgive,' he told her, not hesitating, meaning it. 'A storm came and the wind blew us in different directions is all that happened. I suppose some would call it fate.'

A spark came into her eyes. 'Do you think we could ever – get back together?'

That came as a shock, something he hadn't been prepared for. Vestiges of his old feelings for her were still there but he knew he couldn't give way. Once, a life with her had been part of his dreams. But his time in prison had changed him, stolen things, given him things too. The result was he no longer knew who he was or what he really wanted from life. Explaining it to her would be hard but he'd try.

'Remember that day in the canteen after Prof Deadman's final lecture? Hickson was deriding his views. His point was anyone would do anything given enough self-interest and I said that was rot.'

She frowned. 'I remember, but what has that—'

He held up a hand, interrupted her. 'You could say by my actions I proved Hickson's point.'

She reached for his hand, placed her own over his. 'It's over now, part of the past. You were young, James. We were all young – and naïve. Forgive yourself. I'll help you.'

He removed his hand gently, looked away into the far corner of the room.

'It's not over and I'll never forgive myself. I'll never practise law but I'll find a way to help people in some way and not just for money.' He swallowed the lump in his throat. 'The least I can do is live a useful life for Ted.'

'Together,' she insisted. 'We can do that together.'

He stared into her eyes. 'Right now, when I look at you, you know what I see?'

She narrowed her eyes. 'What?'

'I see you've changed for the better. I can also see Ted's features in your face and I don't think I could live with that –yet.' Picking up his pint, he swallowed the remnants. 'I have to find myself and do it alone.'

She started to cry. 'There's no hope, then?'

'Who knows?' he said, with a shrug, and got to his feet. 'It's a crazy life.'

He looked down at her. This meeting hadn't been easy for him because, in spite of everything, he still felt something for her. But he'd told her the truth, the way it was, and was resolved.

'No hard feelings Liz,' he said, then turned his back and walked away.